THE BOYS RETURN

■ ■ ■ ■ ■ ■

THE BOYS RETURN

Phyllis Reynolds Naylor

DELACORTE PRESS

Published by
Delacorte Press
an imprint of
Random House Children's Books
a division of Random House, Inc.
1540 Broadway
New York, New York 10036

Visit us on the Web! www.randomhouse.com/kids
Educators and librarians, for a variety of teaching tools, visit us at
www.randomhouse.com/teachers

Library of Congress Cataloging-in-Publication Data
Naylor, Phyllis Reynolds.
The boys return / Phyllis Reynolds Naylor.
    p. cm.
Sequel to: A traitor among the boys.
Summary: The Benson boys return to Buckman for spring vacation and concoct a prank involving a nonexistent ghost, continuing the practical joke war between the Hatford boys and the Malloy girls.
    ISBN 0-385-32734-X
    [1. Practical jokes—Fiction. 2. Brothers—Fiction. 3. Sisters—Fiction. 4. Ghosts—Fiction.] I. Title.

PZ7.N24 Bor 2001
[Fic]—dc21   00-050944

The text of this book is set in 12-point Adobe Garamond.

Manufactured in the United States of America

September 2001

10 9 8 7 6 5 4 3 2 1

BVG

To Eric Horwitz

Contents

■　■　■　■　■　■

Cast of Characters

The Hatford Family

Tom Hatford   Father
Ellen Hatford   Mother
Jake and Josh   Sixth-grade twins
Wally   Fourth grade
Peter   Second grade

The Malloy Family

Coach George Malloy   Father
Jean Malloy   Mother
Eddie   Sixth grade
Beth   Fifth grade
Caroline   Fourth grade

The Benson Family

Coach Hal Benson   Father
Shirley Benson   Mother
Steve   Seventh grade
Tony   Sixth grade
Bill   Fourth grade
Danny   Third grade
Doug   First grade

One

■

Big News

There was still a little snow on the ground, but the West Virginia sky seemed to have more blue than it had a month before, and the wind didn't bite the way it had in the depth of winter. The best thing about March, Wally Hartford thought, was spring vacation— a whole week free of Caroline Malloy poking his back with a pencil, or tickling his neck with a ruler, or whispering "Wal-ly" in his ear.

"Do we still have to hang around with them even when we're on vacation next week?" he asked. He and his brothers stopped on the sidewalk in front of their house and waited for the three Malloy girls to cross the swinging bridge.

Ever since a cougar had been spotted in the neighborhood, the Hatford boys and the Malloy girls had been told to stay together when outside. Wally's

1

parents had been particularly concerned about their youngest, Peter, and the Malloys about their youngest, Caroline. Wally, though, was sure that if a cougar ever tried to take a bite out of Caroline, it would spit her out so fast she wouldn't even know she'd been bitten.

"We're supposed to stay together whenever we're outside," said Peter. "Because of the abaguchie." Before anyone had known what the animal really was, the newspaper had referred to it as the abaguchie, and that was the way people thought of it still.

"So we'll stay inside the whole week," muttered Jake. Jake and Josh, the twins, were the oldest Hatfords and were in sixth grade; Wally was in fourth, and Peter in second. Peter liked being around the Malloy girls, and Josh had actually fallen for Beth—for a short time, anyway. Wally felt as though he could stand them in small doses only, but Jake couldn't stand them much at all.

Down the hill came the girls, their hair blowing in the wind because it was warm enough now to go without caps. They started across the swinging bridge over the Buckman River, which entered town on one side of Island Avenue, looped around under the road bridge to the business district, and flowed back out the other side of the avenue.

Trip-trap, trip-trap, trip-trap, went the girls' feet on the wooden planks. Whenever Wally heard that sound, he envisioned a troll underneath, waiting to gobble them up.

"Hi, Josh! Hi, Jake!" said Beth. Her blond hair was all shiny from her morning shampoo. She was the prettiest one of the sisters, Wally thought. She was also the only one of either family who was in fifth grade; Eddie, her older sister, was in sixth with Jake and Josh, and Caroline was in fourth grade with Wally, even though she was a year younger than he. Caroline was precocious, whatever that meant.

"*Now* that abaguchie won't get us!" Peter sang out happily as the seven kids headed for school.

"What are you guys going to do over spring vacation?" Eddie asked. Her real name was Edith Ann, but anyone who called her that was likely to get a sock on the arm. "*I'm* going to be practicing for baseball tryouts."

Jake moaned under his breath. That was what he was planning on doing too.

"*I'm* going to write a book!" declared Beth. "It's going to have chapters and everything. I'm calling it *The Ghoul from the Ghostly Garage.*"

"That was *me*! I was the ghoul in the garage last month, right, Beth? Are you writing a book about me?" cried Caroline, hopping up and down while she walked backward, facing her sisters.

Why was it, Wally wondered, that every time Caroline opened her mouth, she was talking about herself?

"No, it's not about you and it's not about last month. The ghoul is a creature entirely from my own imagination," Beth explained.

3

"I could draw the pictures for you," Josh offered.

"Perfect!" said Beth. Everyone knew that Josh was the best artist in the school.

"And *I* could color them for you," said Peter.

That left Wally and Caroline.

"*I'm* going to practice my voices," said Caroline, who wanted to be an actress. She was still walking backward, and glanced around from time to time so she wouldn't bump into anything.

"What voices are those?" laughed Jake. "Donald Duck? Mickey Mouse? *Tweety* Bird?"

Caroline gave him a haughty look. "I'm going to practice reading *Tom Sawyer* out loud. I'll be all the characters myself—Tom Sawyer, Huckleberry Finn, Becky Thatcher, Aunt Polly, Injun Joe—" Suddenly her left foot went off the curb, and she tumbled into the street.

The boys guffawed, but Caroline was laughing too as she picked herself up. Laughing at her wasn't much fun, Wally realized, if Caroline didn't throw her usual fit.

■

Once inside the school, they all headed for their own classrooms, and Wally took his assigned desk in the front row, right smack in front of Caroline.

"Well, class," said Miss Applebaum. "Let me tell you what I want you to do over spring vacation, so you can be thinking about it."

A low moan went around the room. The last thing

Wally Hatford wanted to hear was that he'd have homework during vacation.

"It's not as bad as all that," said their teacher. "I want you to try something you have never done before, and you decide what that will be. A book you've never read, perhaps; a piece you've never tried on the piano. Maybe you'll learn to Rollerblade, or play the drums, or fly a kite, or make a cake. Be an adventurer! Try something new and tell us about it when you come back."

Now, *that* was the kind of assignment Wally liked. Smiles traveled around the room.

"All *right*!" Wally said, grinning, and Miss Applebaum smiled.

"You sound as though you already know what you want to do, Wally," she said.

Sure, he thought. Eat an entire half gallon of superfudge ice cream all by himself; stay up until one in the morning watching *Batman* reruns; put a muzzle on Caroline Malloy . . . But what he said was, "Not really."

What Wally liked to do most was absolutely nothing—nothing as far as anyone else could see, that is. But a lot was going on inside his head all the while. He could be perfectly content for an hour lying on his stomach on the porch, watching ants going in and out of an anthill on the ground below. How did they know who went where? he would wonder. Did they take turns, or what? Were they all cousins?

Or he could sit at a fogged-up window and make designs on it with his tongue. He had discovered that if he licked off little round holes in the fog and connected them in just the right way, it would look like a bear's paw print. But always, always, just when he was having the most fun, somebody would come along and say, "What are you *doing,* you dork?" and "Hey, Mom, Wally's sitting here licking the window!" And then he'd have to get up and act busy.

No, if Wally had his way, he would spend spring vacation doing nothing whatsoever.

■

When the boys got home from school that day, after leaving the girls at the bridge, they gathered in the kitchen as usual for a snack. They were passing around the cheese crackers and peanut butter when the phone rang. Their mother, of course. She always called from the hardware store to be sure that they'd gotten home okay, and that there wasn't an ax murderer waiting to kill them.

"Hi, Mom," said Wally, his mouth full of cracker. "Everyone's fine."

"Well, that's good, because I have some interesting news," said Mrs. Hatford. Wally could hear customers' voices in the background, and the sound of someone pouring nails into the measuring scoop on the scales.

"We're having pizza for dinner?" Wally guessed.

"Better than that."

"Better than *pizza*?" Wally said. Jake, Josh, and

Peter stopped chewing and began watching their brother's face. "A new car?" Wally guessed.

"Even better than that," said his mother. "I got a phone call from Mrs. Benson today, and they're coming to spend spring vacation in Buckman."

"*What?*" yelled Wally. "*The Bensons?*"

"The *Bensons!*" yelled Jake and Josh.

"They're coming back for spring vacation!" Wally told his brothers, and the kitchen erupted in cheers.

Jake grabbed the phone out of Wally's hands. "Are they moving back here?" He held the phone away from his ear so they could all hear what their mother was saying.

"We don't know yet. Mr. Benson is going to talk to the college about it."

"Are they staying with *us?*" yelled Josh, trying to get the phone away from Jake.

"Mr. and Mrs. Benson are staying at a motel, but I said the boys could bunk with us."

More cheers.

"I have to go. I have a customer," Mrs. Hatford said. "Be good, and we'll talk some more when I get home."

But there was already a parade in progress. Jake went marching around the kitchen like a prizefighter, fists in the air, and Peter followed, banging a knife against the peanut butter jar. Josh did a little dance of joy, and Wally just stood there, a silly grin on his face.

1

It was because Coach Benson had taken a one-year exchange position down in Georgia, moving his family there with him, that the Malloys had come here in the first place. Coach Malloy had taken over Mr. Benson's job for a year and moved *his* family—his wife and three daughters—to Buckman, replacing the best friends the Hatfords had ever had.

"Now the guys will get to see what the Whomper, the Weirdo, and the Crazie are really like," said Jake, gloating. "Man, we're going to have fun! With Bill and Danny and Steve and Tony and Doug, we'll run rings around those girls!"

"We get Steve and Tony!" said Josh, choosing the two older Benson boys. "They get to sleep in our room."

"I want Bill and Danny," said Wally.

"That leaves Doug. Dougie can sleep with you, Peter," said Josh.

"There will be sleeping bags all over the place!" said Wally happily.

"And eleven people around the table at night," said Jake.

"We'll do all the stuff we haven't been able to do since the girls moved in," said Wally.

"Like what?" asked Peter.

The room fell suddenly quiet as the Hatford boys tried to think of just what it was they missed doing since the Bensons had gone away.

"I don't know. Just stuff," Wally said.

He didn't know yet what it would be, but he was absolutely sure that sometime, while the Bensons were here, he'd be able to think of something to try that he had never done before. Spring vacation was beginning to look very good indeed.

■ ■ ■ ■ ■ ■ ■ ■ ■ ■ ■

Two

■

Home Decorating

When Caroline walked down the hill behind their house with Beth and Eddie the next day, she was thinking about the special assignment Miss Applebaum had given the class. Caroline didn't want to do just any old thing she had never done before. It had to be something great.

Her sisters suddenly stopped before crossing the bridge.

"What's wrong?" Caroline asked.

"Get a look at *them*!" Eddie exclaimed.

Caroline's gaze followed her sister's, across the river to where the Hatford boys were waiting for them on the other side, their faces stretched into wide, toothy grins.

"They look like they did when they brought a worm over on Thanksgiving and passed it around the table with the turkey," said Beth.

"They look like they did when we had that snowball fight last winter," said Eddie.

But Caroline thought the Hatford boys looked like they did when they'd tried to toss her in the river, or locked her in the toolshed, or cornered her by the fence in their backyard.

"Well, whatever they're up to, they're just dying to tell us about it, so we might as well get it over with," said Beth. The girls started across the swinging footbridge.

"Guess what?" chortled Jake as soon as they reached the other side.

"I can't imagine," said Eddie. "You're going to move away, I hope? Leave Buckman?"

"Ha! Don't you wish!" said Jake.

"The Bensons are coming back!" said Josh.

"For spring vacation!" said Wally. "They're going to stay with us!"

"And we're going to run rings around you!" boasted Peter, parroting his brothers.

Eddie's eyes narrowed and her upper lip began to curl. "Oh, you are, are you? You and who else?"

"All five Benson brothers, that's who!" said Wally. "Bill, Danny, Steve, Tony, and Doug!"

"Ha!" scoffed Eddie.

"We're *so* impressed!" Caroline hooted.

"I can't wait to meet the mighty Bensons! They're all you guys ever talk about," said Beth as they trooped off toward the school. The older ones made sure that Peter, as the youngest, was walking in front of them—

in case the cougar was lurking nearby, waiting to grab the smallest, weakest one of the bunch.

"Well, wait till they get here. We used to have more fun than a barrel of monkeys when they were around," said Jake.

"More fun than howling outside our windows when our folks were away?" asked Caroline.

"More fun than wolfing down the pumpkin chiffon pie Mom sent over for your mother?" asked Beth.

"More fun than demolishing our snow fort out on the river?" asked Eddie. "So, what are you going to do with your Benson buddies? Run the town?"

"*Lots* of stuff," said Wally.

"Name one thing you can do with them that you can't do with us," said Beth.

"Uh . . . just *stuff*!" said Jake.

"Ha!" said Eddie again.

■

After the girls got home that afternoon, they told their mother that the Bensons were coming back for spring vacation.

"Oh, dear!" she said. "I hope they don't want to see inside the house. I really haven't had time to clean it properly the past couple of weeks."

Caroline took off her jacket and hung it on a hook by the door. "Why would they want to see inside the house?" she asked.

"Because it's their house. We're only renting it, remember? Maybe they'll want to be sure we're taking good care of it—I don't know. I suppose it would be polite to invite them over."

Upstairs in Beth's bedroom, Eddie looked at the racing-car wallpaper and said, "I've got a wonderful idea! Just in case they *do* want to snoop around up here, let's be ready."

"How?" asked Caroline.

"You know what those guys are afraid of most, I'll bet? That we'll turn their bedrooms all around. Let's go out and find all the girly stuff we possibly can and put it up just for spring vacation."

Beth and Caroline laughed out loud.

"Frilly lampshades!" said Beth.

"China dolls!" said Caroline.

"Bows and ribbons and ruffles and lace!" said Eddie. "When those guys get a glimpse of their rooms, it will be heart-attack city for sure!"

They went back downstairs.

"We're going downtown, Mom," Eddie called. "Back in a little while."

"All right, but stay together," Mrs. Malloy called from the dining room. "Keep Caroline between you, and make sure you're home before dark."

The girls put on their jackets and went down the sidewalk to the bridge connecting Island Avenue to the business district.

Once on the other side, they passed city hall and the police department, the bank and the hardware store, and continued past the Dairy Queen. They opened the door to the wallpaper store.

Eddie did the talking. "Do you have any leftover pieces of wallpaper we could buy that won't cost very much?" she asked the owner.

"Well, not enough to paper a room, I'm afraid," the man said. "Just odd pieces. What are you looking for, exactly?"

"Something to go in a girl's bedroom," Eddie told him.

"Look in that barrel back there by the stockroom," the owner said, pointing. "You're welcome to anything you find in there, at a dollar a roll."

The girls found the barrel with an odd assortment of wallpaper rolls sticking out the top.

"Ballet slippers!" said Beth, unrolling one of them. It was a pale blue paper with pink ballet slippers pointed at various angles and a lavender ribbon connecting one to the other, like flowers on a vine.

Eddie rummaged among the rolls until she found one that had pink hearts against a white background, with the word LOVE in red, on each heart.

"Oh, we've got to get that one too!" said Beth. "It will drive them absolutely nuts."

Caroline had not found anything yet for her room, and her sisters helped her hunt until they came across a strip of yellow paper with china dolls on it, each one dressed in a fancy costume and holding a tiny teddy bear.

The Malloys could hardly keep from laughing out loud.

"How much?" Eddie asked at the counter.

The man measured them out. "Tell you what, all you've got here are bits and pieces. What if I said a dollar will cover the lot?"

"Sold," said Eddie.

Next stop was the dollar store. There they found several bushel baskets of marked-down merchandise—a little soiled, a bit worn, but good enough for their purpose. They spent three dollars and fifty cents on ribbon, lace, bows, hearts, sparkles, spangles, and beads.

■

For two evenings the girls worked in their rooms, carefully fastening the strips of wallpaper to the wall with straight pins. When they were done, the room with the racing-car paper had a strip of hearts and ribbon down the middle; the room with football wallpaper had a panel of ballet slippers, and the last room, which had been decorated with wallpaper full of marching toy soldiers, now had a strip of china dolls all along the window.

Every picture in every room had a ruffle around it. Every lampshade was trimmed in lace. Every bedpost had a bow attached; there were beads hanging from light fixtures, and sparkles and spangles glistened on every mirror.

The girls went from room to room admiring their handiwork.

"Isn't it *awful*!" breathed Eddie, pausing in the doorway of her own room.

"Atrocious!" Beth agreed. "Do you think we can stand it for a whole week?"

But Caroline rather liked the idea of sleeping in the middle of all this stuff. It was almost like being on a stage set, surrounded by artificial walls and windows. If Caroline had her way, she would spend the whole week of vacation pretending to be onstage. Every person she met would be a character in a play. She, of course, would say her lines perfectly: *How do you do, Mrs. Hatford? Isn't it a splendid, splendid day?* or *Oh, my poor, darling Peter, to be orphaned at so young an age!*

She would cry, she would laugh, she would rage, she would . . . yes, love! And when her performance was over, the audience would give her a standing ovation and throw roses at her feet.

"After all this work, those Bensons *better* want to come over here and take a look at how we're keeping their rooms," said Beth.

"If they don't, we'll have to lure them here," said Eddie. "We didn't go to all this work and expense for nothing."

Caroline was quiet for a moment. "If *we're* doing all this work to annoy the guys, what do you suppose *they're* up to, to trick *us*?"

But Beth was thoughtful too. "What if they turn out to be nice?"

"Ha!" said Eddie. "All we've heard since we moved to Buckman is the trouble we'd be in for if the Bensons came back—the wonderful Bensons—the best friends the Hatfords ever had. I'm tired of listening to the guys talk about the mighty Bensons. I can't wait to meet them, and I guarantee that whatever they dish out, we can take, and *then* some!"

■ ■ ■ ■ ■ ■ ■ ■ ■ ■ ■ ■

Three

■

Bill and Danny and Steve
and Tony and Doug

Nothing much got done on the last day of school before spring vacation. There was a spelling bee in the
morning, and a video of Australia before lunch, and in
the afternoon, Miss Applebaum passed around pictures of her nieces and nephews.

But just before the final bell she said, "Remember,
class, when you come back after spring vacation, I
want to hear that each of you tried something you've
never done before." And then she added quickly,
"With your parents' permission, of course."

Wally had liked it better the first time she'd said
it, without the "parents' permission" stuff. There
were a lot of whoops and shouts and laughter when
the doors opened at last. All the students poured outside, ready to say goodbye to winter and welcome
spring.

The Hatfords, however, were getting ready to welcome someone else—the Benson boys, who would be arriving the following day with their parents. Mrs. Hatford had already borrowed cots and air mattresses from the neighbors to make beds for five more boys in the house.

At breakfast that morning, Mr. Hatford, in his postal worker's uniform, had sat at the breakfast table and said, "Ellen, do you think we're crazy to have nine boys in the house with us for a week?"

"Probably," Mrs. Hatford had replied. "But it's what might happen when you and I aren't here, Tom, that worries me most. So I told the store I'd be working only half days next week."

"Wise move," her husband had said.

"I figure the kids will be up late every night and will be sleeping in each morning. So I'm going to work from eight till one, then come home and get lunch for everybody. I don't think they can get in too much trouble in the hour or so after they first get up, can they?"

"I'm going to pretend you didn't say that," Mr. Hatford had said, and he'd kissed her on the cheek and headed for the door.

They had acted as though Wally weren't even sitting at the table with them eating his cornflakes, mostly because Wally's eyes were always half closed at breakfast. But he had heard and remembered everything they said. What was going through *his* mind at that moment was, *If I'm going to try something I've never done before, I'd better do it between eight and one o'clock, before Mom gets home.*

■

When the dark green van pulled into the Hatfords' driveway Saturday afternoon, the Hatford boys swarmed outside and almost pulled their friends out of the rear seats, yelling and punching each other and chasing the newcomers around the house.

Wally liked Bill Benson the best because they were the same age and they both knew what it was like to be the middle boy in a large family. Bill was a little pudgy and he was always good-natured, just like his brother Danny, a year younger, who had Bill's round face and blue eyes and was even more chubby. The three of them used to do things together when the Bensons lived in Buckman.

Steve and Tony were closest in age to Jake and Josh. The twins, however, were string-bean skinny, while Steve was broad-shouldered and short, and Tony was broad-shouldered and tall. All four boys could eat three hamburgers apiece and a load of fries without even stopping to burp. Steve was in seventh grade already, but Tony and the Hatford twins would soon be twelve.

Doug was the youngest, a year younger than Peter. He was a small boy with hair so blond it almost looked white.

"How *are* you? How was the trip up?" asked Mrs. Hatford, embracing Mrs. Benson while the two men shook hands.

"Well, it's good to be out of that van," Mrs. Benson said. "Hal and I will be going on to the motel later, but we thought we'd stay a little while to chat and help the boys get settled."

"You're certainly staying for dinner!" said Mrs. Hatford.

"Well, that would be lovely," Mrs. Benson said. "You know what I would really like to do? Stroll over to our old house and see how it looks."

"Well, you're in luck, Shirley, because Jean Malloy called just this morning and invited us all to tea," Wally's mother said. "Tea and cookies, she said. And I thought you might enjoy a little walk after your long trip up from Georgia."

Wally elbowed Bill and saw Jake and Josh exchanging looks with Steve and Tony.

"You mean we finally get to meet the weirdos?" whispered Bill.

"Yep. The Whomper, the Weirdo, and the Crazie, up close in living color," Wally replied.

"In their natural habitat!" added Josh.

"Yeah, Mom, let's go over there," said Steve loudly. "I'd just *love* some tea and cookies."

His mother looked at him suspiciously.

"They make *good* cookies, too!" said Peter, nodding emphatically. "You want some cookies, Dougie?"

Doug Benson nodded his almost-white head.

"Just let me get all the bags upstairs and clean up a bit," said Mr. Benson, reaching into the back of the

21

van for some of the suitcases. Mr. Hatford took two of them and started for the house.

"I'll call and let the Malloys know we're coming," said Mrs. Hatford.

Upstairs, the boys ran from room to room, seeing where each of them was going to sleep, pulling things out of suitcases, trading comic books, and throwing underpants at each other. When Jake and Josh closed the door of their room after Tony and Steve were inside, however, Wally knew they must be planning something. Whatever it was, he wanted to be in on it.

"Come on," he said to Bill and Danny, and the three boys converged on the twins' bedroom.

At first Jake wasn't going to let them in, but after he peeked outside to make sure Peter and Doug weren't there, he let Wally and the two chubby Benson boys into the room. Then he locked the door.

"Tony's got a great idea," Josh said. "Listen."

Tony was sitting on the edge of Josh's bed, his feet on one of the army cots Mrs. Hatford had put in the room. "We've been thinking how we could help you get back at the girls for all the stuff they've done to you," he said. "The snowballs down the neck, the pencil poking in Wally's back . . ."

"The way they turned Peter into a spy . . . ," said Steve.

"Caroline making you think she was rabid," said Danny.

"And the time she put lima beans in the brownies," said Bill.

Tony's grin widened. "What we're going to do, see, is make them think our old house is haunted."

Wally made a face. "They'll never fall for it. Eddie in particular."

"Don't be so sure," Tony said mysteriously, and he took a folded piece of paper out of his pocket. It looked as though it were a hundred years old. "Handle it gently," he said, giving it to Wally.

The paper was yellowed and the edges raggedy. One edge, in fact, was torn as though it had been ripped from a notebook. The brown ink was blurred, and the words seemed to have been written with an old quill pen; there were stains in the center of the page.

March 23, 1867, it said in the upper right corner. The date was so faint that Wally could hardly read it.

"Read it out loud," Tony urged him, so Wally cleared his throat and began:

> *"Yesterday was one of the saddest days of my life here on Island Avenue, and I am so overcome with grief that I hardly know what I am about. My sister, Annabelle, was found in the river yesterday, having gone down with me to see the high water. Her guardian angel must have deserted her, for her foot slipped and the swirling water carried her away before I could grab her.*

Oh, the look on her face as she cried out to me has burned its image on my heart!

"I ran along the riverbank as far as the road bridge, screaming as I went, but no one came in time and the water carried her under. She was found later on the other side of Island Avenue, caught in the brush along shore.

"Her body lies in the parlor now as neighbors come to call, a candle at her head and feet, and my eyes are so swollen from crying I durst not let them see me.

"But strangest of all, I know that Annabelle is with me yet. For when we used to lie together in our bed of a morning, we would sometimes amuse ourselves by each, in turn, rapping out a rhythm of an unnamed song on the wall behind our heads, the other to guess what song it might be.

"And late last night, after her body was laid out in her black dress and lace collar, I went to my room and was startled to hear the tap, tappity, tap of a song—a song I know well, and my blood ran cold to hear it: 'I'll Take You Home Again, Kathleen.' She used to tap out that song for me to guess, my own name being Kathleen, and it *pleased me much. But it pleases me no more, for I can only guess that, because I could not save her, she will come again in the night for me, to take me with her."*

Wally stared hard at the piece of paper after he'd finished reading, and then at Tony. Jake and Josh were staring too, their lips parted, eyes huge.

"Where did you find that?" Jake asked.

"In the wall of my room when we used to live where the Malloys are now, of course," said Tony.

"What? You never told us about it!"

"That's because it never happened," Tony said, trying hard, it seemed, not to smile.

"What?" said Josh.

Steve and Tony burst into laughter, and Tony had to explain. "I got a kit for my birthday that will make any piece of paper look old. It's got ink and a quill pen, and when you write something, you brush this kind of liquid over the paper and stick it in the oven for ten minutes, and it turns yellow, and spots appear."

"But . . . the words! *'I durst not let them see me.'* No one talks like that anymore, Tony. How could you make that up?"

"I know. I copied it out of a book and changed the words around a little, adding 'Island Avenue,' for one thing."

"How did you come up with the title of that song?" asked Wally.

"My grandmother used to sing it. It's supposed to be a love song, I think—'I'll Take You Home Again, Kathleen'—but it sounds sort of spooky if a ghost says it."

Jake's mind was already at work. "Okay. So you're going to tell the girls you found a page out of a diary in your wall when you lived there. Caroline's in your room now. How are you going to convince even her that there's a ghost hanging around?"

"I've got it all figured out," said Tony, and his brothers grinned.

■ ■ ■ ■ ■ ■ ■ ■ ■ ■ ■ ■

Four

■

Pleased to Meet You

Caroline had just gone into the bathroom to brush her teeth—the Hatfords were bringing the Bensons to tea in half an hour—when she heard a startled shriek from the hallway.

She realized she had not shut her bedroom door after her, and now it was too late. She stuck her head out the bathroom doorway.

Mrs. Malloy was standing with one hand over her mouth, staring into Caroline's bedroom. Then, in rapid succession, she opened first Beth's door and then Eddie's, emitting a shriek each time she looked inside.

"Caroline Lenore! Bethany Sue! Edith Ann!" she cried, going back to Caroline's bedroom and starting the procedure all over again. Eddie came out of her bedroom and Beth came warily upstairs.

"What are you trying to do? Drive me out of my

mind?" cried their mother. "I've spent the whole morning cleaning, the Bensons will be here in half an hour, and *look* what you've done to their bedrooms!"

"They're *our* bedrooms right now, Mom, and besides, none of this stuff is permanent," Eddie explained.

Coach Malloy came upstairs to put on his shoes. He tried not to smile as he looked where his wife was pointing and took in the lampshades, the ruffles, the beads, the wallpaper . . .

"Take this stuff down this minute!" Mrs. Malloy ordered.

"*Mother!* They're *our* rooms!" Beth protested.

Mrs. Malloy turned helplessly toward her husband. "They did this on purpose just to annoy those boys!" she said.

Now Mr. Malloy couldn't hold back his smile. "Well, I'd say they're going to succeed very well, but it's only a joke, Jean. And Eddie said all the stuff can come down—it's not glued on. You did promise them, when we moved here, that they could decorate their rooms any way they wanted, you know."

"Whose side are *you* on?" cried Mrs. Malloy.

"The side of reason and sanity, peace and quiet," he answered, going into the bedroom to finish dressing.

"Well, I just hope nobody has to come up here to use the bathroom!" Mrs. Malloy grumbled, going back downstairs. "If we can keep everyone down there, at least *that's* presentable." She turned around. "And for heaven's sake, girls, keep those doors closed!"

Caroline, Beth, and Eddie didn't at all mind keeping their doors closed, because they knew two things: One, the Benson boys wouldn't be able to resist sneaking upstairs to see what the Malloy girls had done to their rooms; and two, when they discovered the doors were closed, chances were they would open them only a little anyway, just enough to peek in. The girls had placed their strips of wallpaper in exactly the right places to be seen if their doors were opened about four inches. They made sure that in that first glimpse, every Benson boy would see at least one beaded lampshade, one ruffled picture, one bow, one lacy something-or-other, and that was worth all the work the girls had put into decorating their rooms so atrociously.

■

At two minutes to four the front doorbell rang, and Caroline—dressed in her black velvet dress and patent leather shoes—answered.

There were Mr. and Mrs. Hatford with Mr. and Mrs. Benson and nine smiling boys, enough for a baseball team. The boys looked so scrubbed and angelic she could hardly believe that five of them were the mighty Bensons she had heard so much about. As for the Hatfords, she had never thought they could look angelic either. Suddenly, on impulse, she curtsied as she held open the door. Then she heard one of the Bensons whisper to Wally, "She's the Crazie, right?"

Maybe they weren't so angelic after all.

Mrs. Malloy was coming out of the kitchen, and she hurried forward to shake their hands just as Coach

Malloy came in the back door with two more logs for the fire.

"We're so glad you could come over," she said. "We're certainly enjoying this house, and we thought you might like to have tea in familiar surroundings."

"How good of you to invite us!" said Mrs. Benson as the girls' father took their coats. Mr. Hatford made the introductions.

They all sat primly around the living room, talking about the weather in Georgia and college football. When Caroline and her sisters went out to the kitchen to get the little cakes and sandwiches their mother had prepared, none of them could quite believe how polite and sincere the nine boys seemed. Except for referring to her as the Crazie, which must have been Wally's doing, Caroline said the Bensons were perfect gentlemen.

"And cute!" said Beth.

"Especially Steve," said Eddie.

"Oh, I like Tony," said Beth. "But Danny's got the bluest eyes!"

"Well, if *I* had to choose, I'd take Bill," said Caroline.

"And Dougie's so sweet!" said Beth. "He and Peter make a pair, don't they? I'll bet those Hatfords made up half that stuff they told us about the Bensons—all the things they did with them and how they were going to run rings around us when they came back for spring vacation. That was just talk, that's all it was."

"Yeah, but we don't really know them. Anyone can look angelic for an hour or so," said Eddie.

Caroline took in the dessert plates and napkins while Mrs. Malloy poured the tea, and Beth and Eddie followed with the platters of cakes and sandwiches. Soon everyone was happily munching on cucumber sandwiches, cream cheese on crackers, and little cakes with green or yellow frosting that Mrs. Malloy had bought from Ethel's Bakery.

The most astonishing thing was how rapidly the food was disappearing. Never having had sons, Mrs. Malloy did not know just how much a boy could eat, and she and Caroline and Beth and Eddie stared. It looked as though the platters of food were being attacked by robotic arms that reached out from all sides, arms whose hands were programmed to pluck a cake here, a sandwich there—every fifteen seconds, it seemed, another morsel of food was gone. Mrs. Malloy quickly excused herself and hurried out to the kitchen, followed by the girls.

"They must be starving! They can't have eaten all day!" she whispered.

"That's just the way guys eat, Mom," Eddie told her. "You'd better make some more."

Out came the cucumbers and olives, the cream cheese and the bread. Mrs. Malloy opened the refrigerator wide and put jars of this and that on the table. Beth cut the crusts off a new loaf of bread, sliced each piece diagonally, and smeared cream cheese or mayonnaise on every one.

31

By the time the third serving of food was being devoured and teacups were refilled, Steve Benson said, quite politely, "Excuse me, but could I use your bathroom?"

"Of course," said Coach Malloy. "You know where it is, of course—right at the top of the stairs."

Eddie and Beth exchanged knowing looks. The girls were tempted to tiptoe up the stairs after him just to see his expression when he checked out his room. But they knew that would be extremely rude, and besides, it was time to make still more sandwiches.

As they brought in the platter, however, Danny and Bill were heading for the stairs, and they saw Steve whispering to Tony. When Danny and Bill came back down, Tony and Doug needed the bathroom too, it seemed.

Mrs. Benson looked embarrassed. "It's all that tea, I'm afraid," she said, smiling apologetically.

"Oh, it's quite all right," said Mrs. Malloy, and the three women chatted on about life in Buckman. They talked about the cougar that had been seen from time to time, and what pie was being offered at Ethel's Bakery that month. The men discussed football scores and the blizzard that had blown through Buckman in January.

If Caroline and her sisters expected the boys to be angry because of all the girly stuff hanging in their old bedrooms, however, the boys didn't show it. They each came back downstairs looking somewhat dazed and desperate, but they remained as polite as ever.

"They're not going to say anything about their rooms, just to annoy us!" Eddie whispered to Beth.

"They'll pretend they didn't even peek!" Caroline whispered.

"Do you have any games or stuff in the basement?" Tony asked. "That's where we kept our computer."

Mr. Malloy overheard. "The basement, yes! Excellent idea. Eddie, maybe these boys would like to play table tennis."

The twelve children went down the stairs. Jake and Josh challenged Steve and Tony, and the others gathered around a pachinko game in the corner.

When the four older boys turned their paddles over to the next in line, they sat down on some folding chairs across from the girls.

"You know what?" Tony said softly to Josh, but loudly enough for the girls to hear. "Doesn't Caroline look like Annabelle?"

Josh looked over at Caroline, then back at Tony. "I don't know. What did Annabelle look like?"

"Who's Annabelle?" asked Caroline, but the boys seemed to ignore her.

"The dress, I mean," Tony went on. "Isn't that what she was supposed to be wearing in her coffin? A black dress with a white lace collar? Caroline's got the dress right, anyway."

"Who's Annabelle?" Caroline asked again, more loudly.

Tony apologized and said, "Just somebody we heard

about. Someone who used to live in this house, I think."

"It's possible!" said Caroline. "I was in a play in January about some families that lived in Buckman, and one of the women was named Annabelle."

A look of genuine surprise passed between Tony and Steve and Josh and Jake. Over at the Ping-Pong table, Wally and Bill and Danny stopped playing momentarily, and Peter kept saying, "Come *on*! Come *on*!" But Wally walked over to where the older kids were sitting.

"No kidding!" Steve said at last. "That *is* a coincidence!"

"So how did you know she was wearing a black dress with a lace collar at her funeral?" asked Beth curiously.

"And how did she die?" Eddie wanted to know.

"Oh, it's a long story," Tony said. "Actually, it's a page from a diary I found in the wall of my room when we were living here."

"That's Caroline's room now," said Wally.

"Really? A letter in the wall?" Caroline said, her eyes huge.

Tony nodded. "It's really old. I don't even like to handle it because the edges are crumbling. But if we see you again before we go back to Georgia, maybe I could show it to you. I've got it in my bag."

"But how did she die?" Eddie persisted.

"She drowned," said Steve. "Really tragic. And there's sort of . . . well, a mystery about it."

34

"What?" cried Caroline, Beth, and Eddie together.

Tony nodded toward Peter and Doug, who were the only ones left at the Ping-Pong table. "Better not talk about it here," he said. "We'll show you the page sometime."

■ ■ ■ ■ ■ ■ ■ ■ ■ ■ ■

Five

■

The Plan

On the swinging bridge later, as the Benson and Hatford boys followed their parents home, they gave each other high fives.

"They *bought* it—hook, line, and sinker!" whispered Jake.

"Not exactly," said Steve. "They haven't read the page from the so-called diary yet. But at least they seemed to like us. They didn't hate us, anyway."

"They'll hate us when they see what we did to their rooms," Tony said, grinning.

"What?" asked Wally.

Steve and Tony began to laugh, and Danny and Bill joined in.

"Cross-eyed faces on the ballet slippers, horns on all the hearts, and a mustache on every china doll and teddy bear," said Steve, and they all laughed together.

"Talk about coincidence, though!" said Tony, chuckling. "I just picked the name Annabelle out of my head, and there really was an Annabelle living in Buckman, according to Caroline. Are we lucky, or are we *lucky*!"

Wally didn't see that it mattered one way or the other. So the girls believed that the diary page was real. So what? Aloud he said, "So, then what?"

"Don't you see?" said Tony. "It's only a step from there to believing that the house is haunted."

Wally still didn't get it. It seemed it would take more than a step to go from believing that a girl had drowned to believing the house was haunted.

Josh, too, was having doubts. "No, I *don't* see," he said.

"Wait till we get up in your bedroom. I'll explain it all then," Tony promised.

In the Hatfords' driveway, Mr. and Mrs. Benson said good night. "Now, remember," they said to the Hatfords. "We're taking you all out to dinner Monday night." And then, with instructions to the boys to behave themselves, they got into their van and drove to the motel where they would be staying for the week.

Peter and Doug wanted to trade Pokémon cards and began spreading them out on the dining room table. That gave the older boys a chance to go upstairs and make a plan.

"So here's the deal," said Tony. "I tell the girls that when we lived in that house, I was awakened every night on March twenty-second by the sound of tapping, as though someone were trapped in the wall or something. And then I'll say I'd feel a chill, like a cold draft sweeping through my bedroom, and cold fingers touching my forehead—you get the picture. But it wasn't until two years ago, I'll tell them, when workmen tore out a panel in my wall, that I discovered this page of a diary that someone hid in there."

"And?" said Bill.

"And do you know what Tuesday is?" Tony asked.

"The day after Monday," said Wally. Bill and Danny laughed. That was one reason Wally liked them. They always thought he was funny.

"What *date* it is?" added Steve.

The boys all looked at each other, and then at the Mark McGwire calendar on the wall.

"March twenty-second!" they all said together.

"Riiiiight!" said Tony. "I'm going to tell Caroline that I figure Annabelle's ghost comes back each year on the anniversary of her death, looking for the sister who couldn't save her. But since I'm a guy, not a girl, she leaves me alone. *Caroline,* however . . . ! We've got to convince Caroline that Annabelle is coming for her. We'll have her so psyched on Tuesday that if she hears so much as a pin drop, she'll run from the room screaming."

"They'll always remember the week the Bensons came here and got them scared so silly that no one would sleep in Caroline's room after that," said Steve. "We'll be famous."

"*Nobody's* going to be scared of a story!" said Wally.

"You don't know those girls! It's got to be more than talk."

"It *will* be." Tony grinned. "What if, on Tuesday night, Caroline goes to bed and hears tapping coming from inside her wall?" He looked around the room, and the other boys began to grin.

"And who's going to do the tapping? How are you going to do that without anyone seeing you? Caroline's bedroom is right next to Beth's, remember," said Josh.

"Right! And what's on the other side of Caroline's bedroom?"

"The bathroom," said Jake.

"Right again!" said Tony. "And I just happen to know that if someone is in the basement tapping a rhythm on the water pipes, the sound will travel right upstairs. Caroline will hear it through the wall."

"But you'd still have to get in their basement!" said Wally.

"Right for the third time!" said Tony. "And did you notice that when we were playing table tennis tonight, I complained that it was too warm and opened a basement window? And that, before we went back upstairs, I closed the window but I didn't lock it? *That's* how I'll get in."

"Man, Tony! You think of everything!" Jake said admiringly. "I'll bet they'll *never* forget your visit!"

"Not by a long shot," said Steve.

"You can count on it!" said Danny. "We'll make it sound real."

Wally didn't say any more. He figured he'd just

better keep his mouth shut when he was around the girls, because he'd probably give it away for sure.

■

The next day Mr. and Mrs. Benson drove back to take their family to church, but as soon as the boys had been delivered to the Hatfords again, Mr. and Mrs. Benson went off to visit other friends. Sunday shirts were exchanged for T-shirts, Mrs. Hatford's baked ham dinner was devoured, and all nine boys trooped off to the school's baseball diamond to help Jake and Josh practice for the sixth-grade baseball team, the Buckman Badgers.

It was as though the March sun knew it was the beginning of spring vacation, for it fought its way from behind the clouds and melted what little snow was left on the ground. Water trickled down the gutters in the streets, the breeze was mild, and by the time the boys reached the ball field, they had their jackets off.

But as they stepped inside the chain-link fence, they stopped and stared, for the baseball diamond was already taken. One girl was standing on the pitcher's mound winding up, the second girl was in the batter's box, and the third girl stood behind her, ready to catch the toss.

"Look at that pitcher! Did you ever see anything more ridiculous?" laughed Steve. "That girl couldn't pitch a ball if—"

The pitch *wasn't* much good, but the pitcher *did* get

the ball in the direction of home plate, and in the second before the catcher could get the ball, the bat came forward with a terrific *crack*.

Nine faces turned slowly upward, nine heads swiveled to stare at the ball sailing high over left field. A second later the pitcher was running after it, shouting happily.

"Way to go, Eddie!" the boys heard Beth yell. "You'll show 'em! How could they *not* let you on the team! How would they dare?"

"That's *Eddie* at bat?" gulped Steve, still staring.

"We don't call her the Whomper for nothing," said Wally.

"Man oh man oh man!" breathed Tony. "That girl's got an arm on her like Mark McGwire!"

"Yeah, but if we can get *Eddie* to believe the ghost story, she won't be such a hotshot!" said Jake glumly.

The boys walked over as Beth came back with the ball.

"Well, look who's here," Wally heard Eddie say.

"So, who's winning?" Josh joked.

"We're just helping Eddie practice for tryouts next week," Caroline explained.

But Beth didn't stop at the pitcher's mound. She walked over toward the boys. "Did you bring the page from the diary?" she asked Tony.

"Diary?" he asked innocently.

"The one about Annabelle. I'm dying to see it."

"Oh. Yeah, I've got it, but I thought maybe we could help Eddie practice," Tony said.

But Caroline and Eddie had gathered around too, and Caroline said, "We can do that later. I'd rather see the page."

"We didn't mean to interrupt your practice, Eddie," Steve said politely. "Man, that last hit was a home run for sure."

"Just show us the page!" Eddie said impatiently.

"What page? What are you talking about?" asked Peter, worming his way into the middle of the circle.

Tony motioned toward the school. "Let's go sit on the steps and I'll tell you."

The Malloy sisters and the Hatfords and the Bensons went over to the steps, where Tony pulled the yellowed paper out of his jacket pocket. He handled it gently, unfolding it slowly, and the paper made a dry, crackling sound. Little bits of paper crumbled in his hand.

"Look how *old* it is!" Caroline breathed.

"Okay. Two years ago," Tony began, "an electrician was rewiring our house, and he had to take out a panel in the wall of my room—Caroline's room now—to get the wires through. And this is what I found when I looked inside. It looks like a page from a diary about a girl named Annabelle who lived in our house on Island Avenue, and who drowned in the river on March 22, 1867. It was written by her sister, Kathleen." And then Tony began to read.

There was not a sound from anyone. Peter and Doug sat with their mouths hanging open. And when Tony got to the line, ". . . she will come again in the night for me, to take me with her," Caroline gave a little shriek.

"So? That was a long time ago, Tony," Eddie said.

"I know. That's what I try to tell myself. But to tell you the truth, I wasn't too sad to leave that house and move to Georgia."

"Why?" asked Beth. "Are you trying to tell us you've seen Annabelle's ghost wandering the halls at night?"

"Yeah, Tony! We never saw any ghost!" said Steve, pretending to take the girls' side.

"Neither did we!" said Danny, going along with it.

"No, I didn't see anything either," said Tony, his face serious. "I didn't even *know* about the page from the diary until two years ago. But all the time we lived in that house, I was waked up once a year by a—a tapping sound in the wall. I didn't think anything of it until I found that page from the diary and read about the sisters' tapping out rhythms of songs on the wall. And it was only last year I noticed that it happened on the same day every year. Last year, for the first time, I felt a chill in the room when the tapping began, as though someone was there with me. And then I felt . . . it felt like cold fingers stroking my forehead."

Caroline whimpered.

"It comes the same day every year?" asked Beth. "What day is that?"

"March twenty-second," Tony told her.

"March twenty-second?" Caroline cried in terror. "That's . . . that's . . . !"

"Tuesday!" they all said together.

■ ■ ■ ■ ■ ■ ■ ■ ■ ■ ■ ■

Six

■

March Twenty-second

"I can't believe how nice they are!" Beth said when the girls went home later.

"I can't believe that the girl who wrote the diary slept in *my* room!" said Caroline.

"*I* can't believe it really happened," said Eddie.

Beth turned on her suddenly. "Why are you always such a spoilsport? You always have to find fault with everything!"

Eddie was surprised at the outburst. "It's just that you and Caroline are ready to believe anything, even after the Bensons got in our rooms and marked up our wallpaper. I don't want you to be disappointed."

"Well, I *like* believing in ghosts and things!" said Beth. "I *want* them to be true. It's a great, spooky story! Why *couldn't* it have happened?"

"Let's go in Caroline's room and see," Eddie told her as they started up the stairs.

There was nothing much to see, of course, except the wall with the strip of china doll wallpaper. Every doll and every teddy bear had a big black mustache. Eddie started at one side of the doorway, and—putting the palms of her hands against the wall—walked slowly around the room, moving her arms up and down as though she were making snow angels. She was feeling for cracks or lumps or bumps beneath the wallpaper.

When she had gone all the way around the room and was nearing the doorway again, she suddenly stopped.

"I feel something," she said.

Caroline and Beth hurried over, and Eddie ran one finger down the wall. "Right here," she said.

Caroline felt where Eddie was pointing. There was a definite ridge beneath the wallpaper. As Caroline followed it with her fingers, she found she was tracing a square.

"Just like Tony said!" Beth told them. "It's right by the light switch. He said they removed a panel from the wall, and that's where he found the page from the diary, right behind it."

Eddie almost looked convinced. "Well, I suppose it *could* have happened. It doesn't mean the house is haunted, though, just because Tony found a page out of a diary."

"But what about the tapping sounds, Eddie? And

46

always on March twenty-second?" Caroline said. Suddenly she grabbed Beth's arm on one side of her and Eddie's on the other. "Sleep with me on Tuesday!" she begged.

"All right," Eddie agreed. "And if we hear tapping . . ." At this point Eddie tapped three times on the wall. ". . . and footsteps . . ." Eddie stomped her feet three times.

". . . and a voice saying, 'I'll take you home again, Kathleen . . . ,' " said Beth in her spookiest voice.

". . . we'll say, 'Kathleen's not here, but you can have Caroline!' " finished Eddie. And all three burst out laughing.

■

The boys didn't show up at the baseball diamond at all on Monday, and on Tuesday it began to rain, so the girls didn't go either.

"I wonder what the guys are doing?" Eddie mused, looking bored as she sat by the window.

"I never thought I'd hear that coming from *you*, Eddie!" Beth told her. "The great Edith Ann, missing the *Hatfords*?"

The thing of it was, Caroline realized, the more the boys ignored them—politely, of course—the more her sisters wanted to see them.

"I didn't say I *missed* them. Especially not the Hatfords. I just wondered what they could be doing with the Bensons that's so much fun," Eddie said.

"Probably sitting inside watching TV," said Caroline.

After dinner Beth suggested they go downtown and hang around Oldakers' Bookstore. Everyone liked to go there—sit and read and maybe buy a pop from the little café on one side of the store. If the boys weren't there, they surely would be at the drugstore.

"Stay together, now!" Mrs. Malloy called out as the girls left the house. "I'd feel better if you'd put Caroline between you, and I want you home before eight. In fact, I'd feel a whole lot better if the Hatfords and Bensons were with you. The more kids in a crowd, the better, till that cougar is caught."

"Don't worry," said Eddie. "I've got my hiking boots on. A cougar tries to get Caroline, I'll kick him in the teeth."

They went down the road to the bridge and sure enough, when they were a block away from the bookstore, they saw the nine boys trooping inside.

"Let's act surprised to see them," Beth cautioned. "We certainly don't want them to think we came *looking* for them."

"We especially don't want them to think we *like* them!" said Eddie.

"But we *are* looking for them, and you *do* like them!" Caroline protested. "Why can't we just act real for a change?"

"Because that's part of the fun, and because we'd never hear the end of it," said Eddie.

The girls walked casually into the bookstore, looking up, looking down, and looking sideways—anywhere but straight ahead where the Hatfords and Bensons were gathered around the paperback rack, looking for new books by Jerry Spinelli.

Caroline played her part so well—she pretended to be absorbed in the picture books along one wall—that she stumbled over Wally's feet and went sprawling.

"Are you hurt?" called Mike Oldaker, coming around from behind the counter to help her to her feet.

But Caroline was only conscious of the fact that Danny Benson was helping her up. And right at that moment, Danny Benson seemed to be the most handsome, polite, strong, attractive, wonderful boy in the whole world.

"I'm perfectly fine," she said once she was standing again.

"Well, well, we didn't know you were here!" Eddie said to Steve Benson. "The decorators!"

"Us?" laughed Steve. "Your rooms, you mean? You're the ones who started it!"

But Beth only had eyes for Tony, and was smiling at him with so silly a grin that Eddie had to poke her several times to make her stop staring.

They went to the back of the store—the "tent," they called it, because Mike Oldaker had put up a canopy and there were places to sit and read beneath it.

But Caroline didn't want to read. "We found it!" she told them.

"Found what?" asked Jake.

"The panel you were talking about, Tony!" Beth said hurriedly.

"I felt along the wall until I found a ridge under the wallpaper, and just like you said, there was the shape of a panel—about two feet square—under the light switch," Eddie told them.

"That's where it was," said Tony. "I was there when the electrician took it out. He propped it against the wall and went back outside to get more tools. I was just poking my head inside the wall, seeing what I could see—spiders and sawdust and stuff—and when I looked down, I saw that piece of paper. I haven't told anyone else except us."

"Wow!" said Peter and Doug together.

Caroline laughed excitedly. "Well, just in case there *is* a ghost, just in case Annabelle *does* come looking for the sister who didn't save her, Eddie and Beth are going to sleep in my room with me tonight."

"Good idea," said Steve. "But I still think Tony may have been imagining things."

"We'll see," said Beth. "We'll just see!"

■

Caroline could hardly wait until bedtime, with Eddie on one side of her and Beth on the other, listening for Annabelle's footsteps in the night. Maybe she could use *this* for her school assignment. But better yet, if she ever became a good actress—if she ever saw CAROLINE LENORE MALLOY in lights on Broadway, and had to play the part of a woman terrified half out of her mind by a ghost—then this would be a wonderful experience for her. She would at last know what real live terror felt like.

"We're going to sleep with Caroline," Beth told their mother at ten that evening.

"In that small bed? It's not even big enough for two, much less three!" said Mrs. Malloy.

"We just want to see if we can do it," Beth said. "We may go camping this summer, and we want to see if we could all fit in one small pup tent."

"A tent, yes. At least you can't fall out of a tent," said their mother. "But it's spring vacation. Do whatever you like."

The girls made cinnamon toast and cocoa and carried it up to Caroline's bedroom. They sat on the bed, having their snack and looking through old comic books, then took turns painting each other's fingernails and toenails. After that they recited all the poems they knew, and finally ended up singing songs in three-part harmony.

"Just like Annabelle and her sister used to do. They tapped out the rhythm on their walls," said Eddie.

"Let's do it!" said Caroline.

"No!" said Beth. "We'd bring the ghost here in a minute!"

At last they lay down. They could hardly stop laughing because either Beth or Eddie always seemed to be falling off the edge of the bed. But finally they braced themselves against Caroline. First Beth dropped off to sleep, then Eddie, leaving Caroline squeezed like a sardine in the middle.

The night ticked on. The room was very dark. It was still raining lightly outside. From far off, Caroline could hear the night sounds—a dog barking, a car going along the road—but mostly it was still. Dark and still, with only the sound of rain.

Her legs began to grow heavy, then her arms, and she started to feel as though she were floating. She didn't know what time it was, but she guessed about eleven. Maybe even midnight.

Her eyes closed against the dark and she felt warm and snug and protected with her sisters on either side of her.

Suddenly . . . *Tap, tappity, tap, tap.*

Caroline's eyes opened, but she saw only blackness. Had she heard something or only imagined it?

Tap, tap . . . tappity-tap . . . tap, tap, tap.

Her heart beat so hard it hurt.

"B-B-Beth!" she whispered, but almost no sound came out.

Try to remember how it feels to be so scared! she told herself, but it didn't work.

"Eddie!" she cried, giving her sister a nudge. "Listen!"

"Huh?" mumbled Eddie in a husky voice, and Caroline felt her rise up on one elbow.

"Hear it?" Caroline whispered.

Nothing. Not a sound.

Then, *tap, tappity, tappity, tap-tap-tap.*

"Beth!" Eddie said.

"I heard it too!" whispered Beth.

"Oh, my gosh! It's—it's coming for *me!*" cried Caroline, and she dived down under the covers.

■ ■ ■ ■ ■ ■ ■ ■ ■ ■ ■ ■

Seven

■

In the Moonlight

"**Y**ou're not going anywhere without us!"

Wally stood in the doorway of his brothers' room and faced the four older boys—Jake and Josh, Steve and Tony. Behind him, Danny and Bill Benson were nodding their agreement.

"We can't *all* go over there!" Jake insisted. "There's no point in it! Tony's the only one who's going to crawl in the window."

"So, why are *you* guys all going?" Wally demanded. "Why doesn't Tony go over there by himself?"

"Because somebody has to be the lookout, that's why," said Josh.

"Well, if *you're* all going, *we're* going," Bill insisted.

"There had better be lots of lookouts, one on each side of the house and a couple more to help Tony make his getaway," Wally told them.

"All right, all right, don't have a spaz," said Steve. "But you've got to get out of the house without Mr. and Mrs. Hatford knowing about it."

"And don't let Peter and Doug in on it, either," warned Jake.

"We'll be careful," said Wally. "What time are you going over?"

Tony and Steve exchanged glances, then looked at Jake and Josh. "Oh, around one in the morning," Tony said.

"One in the *morning!*" said Danny. "I can't stay awake that long."

"It's okay. Just go to sleep, then. We'll tell you all about it tomorrow," said Steve.

Wally went back into his own room with Danny and Bill. "I don't think they're going to wait till one in the morning at all," he said. "If they did, it wouldn't be March twenty-second anymore. They're going to sneak over earlier, but they don't want us along."

"Ha!" said Bill. "So what are we going to do?"

"We're going to turn out our light and not make a sound. They'll think we've gone to bed, but the minute we hear them sneak downstairs, we're out of here!" said Wally.

Why was he doing this? Wally wondered. He certainly couldn't use this for the school assignment. Nothing looked so inviting to him as his bed right now, and nothing good ever came of getting mixed up with the Malloys. He should know that by now. But there was something about having Bill and Danny in his room, something about the way the older boys treated them like babies, that made him talk tough.

There was a light tap on the door, and Mrs. Hatford stuck her head inside. "Anything else you need, boys? Peter and Doug are having some popcorn and cocoa downstairs. Want to come down for a snack?"

"I think we'll just bring some popcorn up here, Mom," Wally told her. Even his *mother* was treating them like babies.

"Okay. Help yourselves," she said. The boys heard her tap on Jake and Josh's door too before she went downstairs, but all she asked them was whether they wanted a snack. She didn't offer them popcorn and cocoa. Naturally, they got to choose whatever they wanted!

When Wally went down to the kitchen, Peter and Doug were sitting at the table, swinging their legs and taking turns reaching into the popcorn bowl, their mouths rimmed with marshmallow.

"Hey, Wally!" said Peter. "Doug and me are gonna play Monopoly on my bed. You wanna play?"

"I don't think so," Wally told him. "I'm pretty tired. I think Bill and Danny and I will turn in early."

"Well, *we're* going to stay up till *midnight*!" crowed Doug.

"Yeah. We may not go to sleep all night!" said Peter.

"Good for you," said Wally, and took a bowl of popcorn upstairs with a giant-size bottle of Mountain Dew.

Peter and Doug held out until nine-thirty. Mrs. Benson called, and Doug talked to his mother for a while. Then the two boys took a bath together and had a water fight. After Mrs. Hatford came up to calm them down, they finally went to bed, and the upstairs grew very quiet.

Wally, Danny, and Bill took turns listening at the crack in their door for any sign that the four older boys were leaving the house.

"Dad and Mom go to bed around ten. The guys will wait till they're sure they're asleep, and then they'll leave, I'll bet," said Wally.

Ten-fifteen came, ten-thirty, ten-forty, and there was still no sign of activity from Josh and Jake's room, no light from under their door, no stirrings or rustlings.

"When do you suppose they're going to go?" Bill asked.

"Maybe they fell asleep," said Danny.

Wally went out into the hall. He tiptoed over to his brothers' room. Not a sound. Gently he tried the handle. The door was locked. But his feet were cold, and he realized suddenly that there was a draft coming from under the door.

The window!

He hurried back to his room. "They've already left!" he said. "They climbed out their window and slid down the tree."

Danny and Bill jumped up and pulled on their shoes.

"We've got to be really, really quiet, though," Wally warned. "And don't step on the next-to-last stair from the bottom. It squeaks."

Silently the boys crept out into the hall and down the stairs, careful to avoid the squeaky step. They pulled on their jackets and passed the big clock in the hall, which said 10:44, softly opened the front door, and closed it behind them.

The air was heavy and damp. Occasionally the moon peeped out from behind stormy, swirling clouds, then hid its face again. The boys made their way off the porch and down the sidewalk, where they crossed the road and went down the bank to the swinging bridge.

The boards bounced and the bridge swayed beneath their feet. As they climbed the hill on the other side to the house where the Malloys were staying, they could see no glow in the windows, no light on the porch.

Wally led his friends around the clump of lilac bushes at the edge of the yard, and suddenly, *whump.* He collided with a warm, sturdy body—a body in a nylon jacket smelling of popcorn.

"Hey!" said Wally.

"Hey!" said the jacket.

"Josh?" asked Wally.

"Wally?" asked the jacket.

The boys confronted each other. "I thought you were going to let us know when you came over here," Wally said.

"There was too much noise going on. It took Peter and Doug forever to go to sleep, and we figured if we came through the hallway, someone would see us. So we went out the window," Josh told him.

"Yeah, I'll bet you weren't going to tell us at all!" Bill said.

"Shhh. I'm the lookout here. I have to keep my eyes on Mr. and Mrs. Malloy's bedroom and tell Steve if their light comes on," Josh said.

"Well, we can help!" said Danny.

"Okay, just spread out around the house and watch for a light," Josh said. "Tony's crawling in the basement window right now, and he's going to start tapping. The minute you see a light go on anywhere in the house, give a whistle. Steve will tell Tony, Tony will crawl back out, and we'll all run like heck."

Bill and Danny moved on to the far side of the house, but Wally went around to where Steve and Jake were crouched by the open window, ready to pull Tony to safety at the right moment.

Wally crouched down by the window too.

"What are *you* doing here?" Jake asked irritably.

"Same as you," Wally said. From inside the basement he could hear a faint sound. *Tap . . . tappity . . . tap-tap.*

Steve and Jake grinned at each other.

Tap, tap . . . tappity-tap . . . tap, tap, tap.

Steve couldn't contain a chuckle.

"Do you see any lights coming on?" Jake whispered to Wally.

Wally backed away from the house and scanned the windows. "Nope," he said.

"Tap louder, Tony," Steve whispered, sticking his head in the window. "Maybe no one can hear it."

TAP . . . TAPPITY, TAPPITY, TAP, TAP, TAP, went the rapping on the water pipes, louder still.

"Hey, cut it out, Wally," muttered Jake.

"What?" said Wally.

"Leave me alone," said Jake. "Quit bumping against me."

"I'm not doing anything. I'm clear out here," said Wally. He strained to see Jake in the darkness, and then they saw it. They all saw it: the cougar, sniffing around next to Jake.

"C-c-cougar!" gasped Jake, throwing up his hands and springing backward. The animal turned and sprinted across the yard, disappearing into the trees.

"Cougar!" Steve croaked through the basement window.

A moment later Tony came crawling out, Steve and Jake half dragging him the rest of the way, but he remembered to pull the window closed behind him. Then the boys were racing pell-mell down the hill to the footbridge, Bill and Danny and Wally at their heels, Josh bringing up the rear. They didn't stop till they reached the other side of the river.

"What happened? Did they see you?" Josh asked, breathless.

"No! It was the cougar! Right beside me!" Jake gasped. "I think it touched my neck with its nose!"

"Oh, you're imagining things," said Josh.

"No! I saw it too!" said Steve.

"So did I!" said Wally.

"Man oh man oh man!" said Jake. "I've never been that close to a wild animal in my life! Do you think it was about to attack me?"

"Probably wanted to sniff you out first, see if you'd taste any good," said Steve, trying to make a joke. But no one laughed.

Tony was upset that his little trick on the Malloys seemed to have been preempted by the cougar. "What about the girls?" he asked. "Did a light come on in Caroline's bedroom?"

"No," said Danny. "Maybe nobody heard the tapping."

"Great! So we—" Jake suddenly froze. "L-l-look!" he said.

The boys turned around. There on the hill, on the Malloys' side of the bridge, stood the cougar, bathed in a spot of moonlight. It was standing very, very still. Only its tail was twitching.

■ ■ ■ ■ ■ ■ ■ ■ ■ ■ ■ ■ ■

Eight

■

A Small Suspicion

"Caroline, just shut up and listen!" Eddie whispered. "Is it coming from inside the wall or not?"

"It—it *sounds* like it's coming from the bathroom!" Caroline said shakily.

"Maybe Annabelle likes to tap out a song while she's on the pot," Beth suggested.

"Turn on the light!" Caroline begged.

"No!" Eddie was firm. "If Tony was right, and the ghost just comes around once a year, this is our only chance to find out what it's all about."

Tap . . . tap . . . tappity.

Slowly Eddie got out of bed. One foot touched the floor, then the other. Nothing grabbed her feet.

"Why don't you try talking to Annabelle, Caroline?" Beth suggested. "If she's coming for you, you'd better set her straight."

Caroline inched her way out from under the covers. Beth was right. If she could talk Annabelle out of coming back every March twenty-second—if she could talk to a ghost at *all*—she would be famous even *before* she became a great actress. She would be known far and wide as Caroline Lenore Malloy, the girl who talked to a ghost. Well, she'd be known around school, anyway.

Tappity . . . tappity . . . tap, tap . . . tappity.

Caroline threw off the covers suddenly and sat up.

"Annabelle?" she said, her voice shaking. "The g-girl you're looking for isn't here. I'm C-Caroline, from Ohio, and I didn't have anything to do with your drowning in the river. Your sister really, *really* tried to save you, but she just couldn't reach you in time. In fact, I hate to tell you this, Annabelle, but the truth is . . . well, you're dead, and you really shouldn't be walking around like this."

Tap, tap, tap.

Eddie, Beth, and Caroline grabbed each other in the dark. Now the tapping wasn't just in the wall any longer. It was on the bedroom door!

"A-A-Annabelle?" whispered Beth.

Creeeaak!

The door swung open and there stood Mr. Malloy in his robe, holding a flashlight.

"Caroline, are you having a nightmare, or just talking to yourself?" he asked.

"I was just . . . just rehearsing for a play," Caroline

said. "I mean . . . a play I might possibly be in sometime in the distant future. . . ."

"Well, it's getting close to midnight, and time you girls were asleep, vacation or no vacation," their father said. "If you're going to chatter all night, perhaps you should sleep downstairs."

"We're going to sleep right now," Beth said, knowing she wouldn't sleep on the floor downstairs for anything in the world.

"What woke you up, Dad?" Eddie asked. "We weren't talking *that* loud."

"Actually, I thought I heard a sort of knocking sound," Mr. Malloy said.

"You *did*?" Beth asked. "You mean you heard it too?"

"Yes. It sounded as though it was coming from the bathroom. Could just be air in the pipes or something. Well, you girls pack it in now. Cut the chatter and get some shut-eye, okay?"

"Sure," said Eddie.

The door closed again, and the girls could hear their father's footsteps going back down the hall.

"He heard it too!" said Beth. "Whatever it was, he heard it, so we didn't just imagine things."

"But it's stopped. It must have heard Dad's voice and gone away," said Caroline.

"And it won't come back for a whole year," said Beth, looking at her watch in the dark. "It's now March twenty-third."

"Oh, I *wish* we could have talked to her!" Caroline said. "How do we know she won't be back? Maybe she didn't come back before because she found a boy in her room. Maybe because it's *me,* she'll be here again tomorrow night."

"We'll see. I've got some thinking to do," said Eddie.

■

When Caroline woke up the next morning, there was only one sister in bed with her. Beth, snoring softly, was sprawled on her stomach, one leg over Caroline, but the other side of the bed was empty. Eddie was gone.

Caroline blinked and looked at the clock. Two minutes after ten! She'd slept away half the morning!

She carefully disentangled herself from Beth and padded downstairs in her pajamas and slippers. Mrs. Malloy was making pancakes.

"I guess I'm making breakfast this morning in shifts," she said. "First your father, then Eddie, now you. . . . I suppose Beth's still sleeping?"

"Yes. Where's Eddie?" Caroline asked.

"She was up and out a half hour ago. Said something about going to the library. What are you girls going to do today? It's raining again, so I'm afraid you're going to be stuck inside. I have a meeting of the Faculty Wives' Club this morning."

"I don't know yet," Caroline told her. "Did Eddie say when she'd be back?"

"No. Do you want maple or raspberry syrup, Caroline?"

"Raspberry," said Caroline, and she sat with her head in her hands, trying to figure things out.

Eddie came back around ten-thirty. By that time Beth was up, eating the last of the pancakes. Eddie motioned for her and Caroline to follow and took them both upstairs. When they were in Eddie's room, she closed the door and sat on the edge of her bed.

"It's a fake," she said.

"Annabelle?" asked Beth.

Eddie nodded. "The whole kit and caboodle. Fake! Fake! Fake!"

"How do you know? What about the page from the diary and the tapping?"

"I don't know how Tony got that page, but it's a fraud. And I don't know what made the tapping, but listen to this: The date of the diary entry was March twenty-third. Right? In 1867? And it said that Annabelle had drowned the day before, on March twenty-second. That her sister ran along the bank as far as the road bridge, okay? And then the sister heard Annabelle's ghost singing 'I'll Take You Home Again, Kathleen.' Right?"

"Right," said Beth.

"Fact number one: The song 'I'll Take You Home Again, Kathleen' wasn't written until 1876. I looked it up at the library."

Caroline and Beth sat as still as stones, listening.

"Fact number two: There was no road bridge here in 1867."

Caroline's mouth dropped open, and Beth's eyes widened.

"Fact number three," continued Eddie. "This *house* wasn't here in 1867. Didn't Dad tell us it was ninety years old? Whoever wrote that page from a diary— Tony, I suspect, or maybe *all* the Benson boys—didn't have their facts straight."

Beth wanted to call the boys immediately and call their bluff, but Caroline was clearly disappointed. She had so wanted to believe in a ghost. What a wonderful report this would have made for school! "Then why did Tony go to all that work to make us believe this stuff?" she asked.

"To see if we'd fall for it! Just to have something to tease us about if we did," Eddie said.

"Well, at least we didn't give them the satisfaction of getting hysterical and running out of the house screaming last night," Beth said. "Oooh, I wish we could get back at them somehow."

"We will," said Eddie.

"How?" asked Caroline.

"Well, the next time we see the guys, we've got to act quiet and thoughtful and scared. Got it?"

"Got it," said Beth.

"But we *were* scared, and we *did* hear tapping!" said Caroline.

"I'm coming to that," said Eddie. "They found a way to get in the house last night. It's their house, remember, and they know it better than we do. But we're going to tell them that the ghost came back, all right, because around eleven o'clock, after we had all gone to bed, we heard her calling. We'll tell the guys we were all spending the night in your room, Caroline, waiting for the ghost to show up. We heard a tapping, and saw a pale blue light coming through the wall, and heard a soft, wavery voice saying, 'Where is he? Where is he?' And when we called out, 'Who?' the ghost dropped this at our feet and disappeared." Eddie reached into her pocket and pulled out a horseshoe key chain with several keys attached.

"Where did you get *that*?" asked Caroline.

"Whose *is* it?" asked Beth.

"Tony's, I think," said Eddie, with satisfaction. "Do you remember when we were all down in the basement playing table tennis? Tony was too warm and took off his jacket, and then he opened the window? Well, when he closed it again, he didn't lock it, just so he could get back inside. I went down this morning and checked, and found this on the floor below the window."

"Aha!" said Beth.

"Soooo," Eddie continued, "we're going to make the boys think we're really scared. Because the ghost came back and said she was looking for the owner of a key chain. And *that's* the one she's really after. We'll pretend we don't know what she's talking about." Eddie began to grin, then Beth, then Caroline.

"Those poor dumb boys," said Beth, shaking her head. "They're up against the very best! *Us!*"

■ ■ ■ ■ ■ ■ ■ ■ ■ ■ ■ ■ ■

Nine

■

Trouble

The boys stood breathlessly at their end of the footbridge, staring at the spot on the hill where the cougar had been.

"The sheriff said that if anyone sees the cougar, he's to call his office right away," said Wally.

"Are you nuts?" said Jake. "He'll want to know exactly where and when we saw it. What do we say? That we were outside the Malloys' basement window between eleven and twelve at night?"

"Maybe we should just tell Dad," Wally said nervously.

Now both Jake and Josh turned on him.

"That's even *worse!*" said Josh.

"We were not only at the Malloys' basement window late at night, but we crawled out *our* bedroom window to get there!" Jake said.

There seemed to be nothing left to do but go home and crawl back up the tree.

"What happened after you started tapping on the water pipes?" asked Danny as they made their way up the path, looking over their shoulders from time to time. "Did you hear any footsteps above you?"

"Not really," said Tony. "Did you see any lights come on?"

"No," said the others.

"Well, even if nobody heard the tapping, at least they didn't catch us," said Steve disappointedly. "You closed the basement window again, didn't you, Tony?"

"Sure."

"But you didn't lock it," said Wally.

"Of course not. How could I?"

"Now, remember," said Steve. "We're not going to say one word to the girls about this. Don't even mention March twenty-second. If they *did* hear something and suspect us, that'll really throw them. They'll be waiting to see if we say anything, which would prove us guilty for sure."

"Right!" said Jake. "Don't mention it to Peter or Doug, either. They'll spill the beans the first time they open their mouths."

Trying to get up the tree proved to be a lot more difficult than coming down.

"Why don't we boost Wally up? He can unlock our bedroom door, sneak downstairs, and open the door for the rest of us," Jake suggested. "He's the lightest."

Arrrggghhh! thought Wally. This always happened!

No matter what wild scheme Jake or Josh thought up, it was always Wally who got suckered into doing the dirty work.

"If this is so simple, how come you didn't all go *out* the door to begin with?" Wally asked.

"Because they didn't want *us* to hear them, that's why. They didn't want us along," said Bill.

"Right!" said Danny. "They can just climb up the stupid tree and open the door themselves!"

On the other hand, Wally thought, it *was* cold out here, and there *was* a cougar lurking about, and Wally *was* lighter than either Bill or Danny, and there *was* a half-eaten bowl of popcorn waiting back in Wally's room. If *someone* didn't crawl in the window and open the twins' door from the inside, his brothers would be out here all night.

"Oh, I'll go," he said. "Give me a boost."

Jake and Josh linked arms to form a step, and Wally climbed on top, grabbed the lowest limb of the maple, and shinnied his way to the third branch just outside the twins' window. He felt for the window ledge and then for the open window.

"Hey!" he said. "The window's closed!"

"You jerks!" Jake called up. "You guys must have closed it behind you when you followed us."

"We didn't come through your room!" cried Danny. "Your door was locked, remember? We came down the stairs!"

"Then double duh!" said Steve. "This is a no-brainer. If you came out the front door, then that's the way we'll go back in."

Wally climbed back down the tree, and they walked around to the front of the house.

"Now, remember," said Jake. "When we get inside, the second stair from the bottom really squeaks. You have to step over it."

"If Mom gets up, we'll just say we got hungry and went down to get some crackers or something," said Josh.

The boys went softly onto the porch, and Wally reached for the door handle.

"Wait a minute!" said Jake. "If the window was closed, that means somebody got in our room somehow and closed it after we left!"

"But we locked our door!" said Josh.

"Uh-oh," said Tony.

"Maybe the window slammed down all by itself," said Steve, hugging himself with his arms. "Come on. I'm cold."

Wally tried the door. "*It's* locked!" he said, turning around.

"You jerks!" Steve said, facing the younger boys. "You must have locked it behind you!"

"We did *not*!" Wally insisted. "I made sure it wasn't latched. I'll bet Dad got up and locked it."

"Wait a minute," said Tony. "I've got an old skeleton key. Maybe that will open it." He put his hand in his jacket pocket, and then his jaw dropped. "It's gone!" he said. "My horseshoe key chain is gone!"

"What do you mean, gone?" asked Steve.

"Gone, as in G-O-N-E," Tony said. "It had my bike-lock key on it too, and the key to our house down in Georgia."

"We are in deep, deep doo-doo," said Bill.

Suddenly the porch light came on, the front door opened, and there stood Mr. Hatford in his striped pajamas.

"Well, well, well! How nice to see you!" he said. "Won't you come in? May I offer you something to eat?"

One by one, the seven boys filed into the house, the Bensons with their eyes on the floor, the Hatfords wishing they were anywhere but there.

"H-how did you know we were gone?" Josh asked.

"How did I know you were gone? Well, first of all there was a crash from your room, and when I went to investigate, the door was locked. Nobody came when I knocked. Second, after I got the screwdriver from the basement and got inside, I found your window wide open. The wind had blown a poster down off the wall, and when it fell, it knocked over your soda-can pyramid. It doesn't take much of a brain to figure out just how you guys got out. Though what you did after you got out is something *you'll* have to tell *me*!"

Wally actually felt relieved. Now that their father knew they'd been outside, there was no need to keep the cougar secret.

"We just wanted to go out and horse around," said Josh. "We didn't want to wake anyone."

"Horse around . . . at the Malloys' house, by chance?" asked his dad.

"Well, sort of," said Josh. "I mean, we walked across their yard."

"And did the Malloy girls sort of come outside and horse around with you?"

Wally was surprised to see the older boys blush.

"Of course not!" said Jake. "They didn't even know we were out there."

Wally saw his chance to change the subject. "But, Dad, we saw the cougar again! It came right over to us!"

"Yeah!" said Jake. "It nuzzled my face. It bumped right into me!"

"What?" cried Mr. Hatford.

"It did!" said Jake, glad that the conversation had taken a new direction. "I thought the other guys were fooling around, bumping into me, and when I looked, it was the cougar." His voice was still shaking. "It was like . . . like, sniffing me out or something, and when I yelled, it bolted and ran."

"Boys!" said Mr. Hatford. "You shouldn't have been out there! I'm going to call the sheriff in the morning. He figures it might have been somebody's pet that got away. And if that person didn't have a permit to keep a wild animal, he's not about to report it and get in trouble. That may be why it's hanging around so close to town. Either that or it's getting mighty hungry. You boys get to bed, and we'll have to go over the house rules tomorrow. No more sneaking out at night, or

I'm going to ground you for the whole week. Understood?"

Wally and Jake and Josh nodded.

"And you Bensons too?" Mr. Hatford said.

The Bensons nodded.

"Good," said Mr. Hatford.

Gratefully the seven boys went upstairs. In the twins' bedroom, there were empty Coke and Sprite and Mountain Dew cans scattered all over the floor.

"Well, at least we didn't get in big trouble," said Josh. "Not yet, anyway."

"Yeah? *I'm* in big trouble!" said Tony. "I lost my key chain, and I don't know where to look for it."

■ ■ ■ ■ ■ ■ ■ ■ ■ ■ ■ ■

Ten

■

A Ghostly Gathering

As soon as Mrs. Malloy left for the meeting of the faculty wives, Eddie phoned the Hatfords. The girls had spent an hour up in Beth's room that morning rehearsing just what they were going to say and felt they were as ready as they'd ever be.

There were three rings at the other end before someone answered, and Eddie held the phone away from her ear so that Beth could hear too.

"Hello?" It was Josh's voice.

"Hi, Josh. It's me, Eddie."

Caroline, who was listening in on the phone upstairs, had never heard Eddie talk like that. Her voice was low and soft and scared-sounding, and her words wavered a little at the end.

"Oh. Hi," said Josh. *He* sounded cocky. Confident.

"I just . . . just wanted to say that T-Tony was

right!" Eddie went on. "About March twenty-second, I mean. The house *is* haunted."

Caroline heard muffled voices at the other end of the line, and then a click as though someone was picking up another phone somewhere in the Hatford house. Caroline thought she could hear another person breathing.

"Why? What happened?" Josh said at last, and Caroline could almost see him smiling as he said it.

"Oh, it's just too scary," Eddie continued. "Dad's at the college and Mom's at the faculty wives' meeting, and to tell the truth, we're a little bit scared to be here alone. Do you suppose you guys could come over for a little while?"

Now there were excited whispers at the other end of the line, Caroline was sure of it. Even a muffled laugh. Then Tony took over the phone.

"Eddie? This is Tony. What happened? Did you hear something, or what?"

"Yeah, but *please* come over till Mom gets back. Okay?" Eddie pleaded convincingly.

"Sure. We'll be right there," Tony said, and hung up.

Caroline ran downstairs to her sisters. Eddie, Beth, and Caroline bent over double, laughing.

In no time at all, it seemed, they saw nine boys coming up the hill from the footbridge.

"Look at them," said Beth. "They even brought reinforcements. They've got Peter and Doug with them."

"Okay, now. Get ready. Wipe those smiles off your faces," Eddie said.

The three girls went to the door, looking frightened. It was like being in a play with her sisters, Caroline decided. She wondered if she had ever had so much fun. Well, yes, she had. When they had first moved to Buckman, for example, and they knew the boys were spying on them—when Caroline pretended to be dead, and her sisters had carried her to the river and dumped her body in. Or the time the Hatford boys had locked her in their toolshed, and when they opened the door at last, Caroline had pretended to be rabid. Oh, the stage was where she belonged, most definitely!

The boys, Caroline could see, were trying hard not to smile. All except Peter and Doug, who didn't have to try at all because, to them, there was nothing to laugh about. Obviously, they didn't have a clue.

Beth pulled them quickly inside. "We're *so* glad you're here!" she said. "It's been so scary!"

Tony and Steve were even nicer than they'd been the day before. Everyone sat down in the living room, Peter and Doug with wide eyes, wanting to hear what had happened, and Danny and Bill looking strangest of all because they were trying so hard to keep straight faces. Their mouths kept twisting into grotesque shapes.

"Tell us what happened," said Steve.

"Well," Eddie began, her voice trembling just a little. Caroline was terribly impressed. She'd had no idea her sister was such a good actress. She was even a little envious. "Caroline was afraid to spend the night alone after what Tony told her, so Beth and I got in bed with her, just in case."

Caroline saw Jake nudge Tony almost imperceptibly with his elbow.

Beth took up the story. "Everything was quiet until . . . oh . . . eleven o'clock. Maybe later. And then we heard it!"

"Heard what?" asked Tony. "Did you hear the tapping I told you about?"

"Yes! It was just like you said," Eddie answered. "Sort of *tap, tappity, tap, tap*. It could have been the rhythm of a song."

"It was Annabelle, I know it!" wailed Caroline. She saw Wally and Bill and Danny put their heads down so that no one could see their faces.

"And then," Eddie went on, "it happened!"

The boys jerked to attention. "*What* happened?" asked Tony.

"We saw *her*, of course!" said Beth, wrapping her arms around her body as though to stop the shaking.

"*Who?*" asked Steve and Josh together.

"Annabelle! It had to be her," said Eddie.

"Huh?" said Tony.

"Well, we don't know that for sure," said Beth, "but it had the shape of a young girl, and the—"

"*What* did?" the boys cried together.

"The pale blue light," said Eddie. "It was coming right through the wall where the—"

"Wait a minute, wait a minute!" said Tony. "First you heard a tapping, and then . . . ?"

Beth and Caroline nodded.

"But just before midnight," Eddie went on, her eyes huge, "there was this light, this pale blue light."

Caroline took over again. "We all sat up together to see where it was coming from, and right out of the wall, where the old panel had been, came this blue light—first her head, then her body, her arms and legs . . ."

"But it was her *voice* that I'll never forget as long as I live," cried Beth, covering her face with her hands.

"What did she say?" gasped Peter.

"It was more like a wail," said Caroline.

"No, like a . . . a moan," Beth said.

"No, it wasn't. It was a screech! An angry screech," Eddie insisted. "And she kept saying the same thing over and over: '*Oh*-nee! *Oh*-nee!' "

"*Oh*-nee?" asked Steve. "What was she? An Indian?" The boys tried to laugh but didn't succeed.

"It was hard to make out *what* she was. But if I had to guess, I'd say a young girl. I couldn't tell anything else. A young girl in pain," said Eddie.

"But she . . . the light . . . just kept looking all around and wailing, as though we weren't even there," said Caroline.

Beth took up the story. "We kept asking her, 'What do you want? Maybe we can help you,' but all she said was, 'Where is he? Where is he?' "

"Then what?" asked Wally, his eyes unblinking, his lips so dry they stuck together.

"Then the light moved all around the room, like . . . like she was looking for something," said Eddie.

"Or somebody," said Caroline.

"And then . . . *then* she cried, '*Oh*-nee!' and disappeared," said Beth.

"But this is the spooky part," Eddie told them. "As soon as the blue light faded away, we turned on the light. . . ."

"We were so *scared*!" Caroline shivered.

"And right where the blue light had been, we found this," said Eddie. She held out her hands and unfolded her fingers. There lay a horseshoe key chain with several keys attached.

Tony's mouth fell open. "It's—it's mine," he said.

The girls looked at him in mock horror.

"Yours?" said Caroline.

"She must have been saying 'To-ny! To-ny!' " said Wally softly.

The boys looked at each other, not quite believing, then at the girls.

And suddenly, from somewhere in the house, came a *thunka . . . thunka . . . thunka . . . thunka. . . .*

"The ghost!" yelled Peter, and he dived behind the couch.

■ ■ ■ ■ ■ ■ ■ ■ ■ ■ ■ ■

Eleven

■

What Next?

What were he and his brothers and friends doing over here? Wally wondered. Why did all their tricks on the girls seem to backfire? There probably *was* a girl named Annabelle who had once drowned in the Buckman River; there probably *was* a sister who had failed to save her and who lived in the Bensons' old house. So there probably was a *ghost*, too, and here it was, in that very house where the *thunka, thunka, thunka* came again.

"J-J-Jake," he said, "maybe we should go home."

"Don't leave us!" cried Caroline. "That was for *real*!"

"Caroline!" yelled Eddie.

"You mean this other stuff was all a joke?" asked Steve.

Thunka . . . thunka . . . thunka . . . came from the

walls again, and then the sounds of soft footsteps coming around the side of the house.

Peter and Doug were both behind the sofa now.

Suddenly . . . *knock, knock, knock.*

Caroline felt as though she had risen three inches off her chair.

"Wh-who's going to answer?" asked Tony.

Knock, knock, knock, came the sound again.

Eddie slowly got up from the sofa. She moved noiselessly across the rug and out into the hallway. And finally, taking a deep breath, she grasped the doorknob and pulled open the door.

A deep voice said, "Malloy?" And as the Malloys and Hatfords and Bensons gathered behind her, Eddie found herself looking into the shadowed face of a man in a dark uniform and cap.

"Y-yes?" Eddie said.

"Upshur County Water and Sewer," the man said. "Your dad called this morning about noise in the water pipes, and I just bled the air out of them at the meter. I think they'll be okay now. You can tell him."

"Okay," said Eddie, relief showing in her voice. She closed the door and turned to face the others.

"Of course! Air in the pipes. *We* knew that!" bragged Tony.

"We saw them do that once out in our yard," said Steve.

"Well, if you knew that noise was just the utility company draining air from the pipes, why didn't you say so?" Eddie demanded. "You were just as scared as we were. And *you* thought you could scare *us*!"

"What do you mean?" asked Tony.

"Ha!" said Beth. "'I'll Take You Home Again, Kathleen,' my eye!"

"Huh?" said Steve.

"All that talk of a drowning in 1867, and somebody singing that song . . . the song wasn't even written till 1876. I checked," said Eddie.

"And Annabelle's body was found near the road bridge, my foot!" said Caroline.

"It *was*!" said Tony.

"The road bridge wasn't even there in 1867," said Eddie. "I checked that too. And this *house* wasn't here in 1867 either! Your story has more holes than Swiss cheese, Tony Benson!"

The boys started to grin.

"But we had you going, didn't we?" laughed Steve, playfully swatting at her with a newspaper. "Sort of had you wired? Psyched? You were scared enough that you were all three squeezed into one little bed. You said so yourself."

"And we had *you* going when I told you Annabelle had your horseshoe key chain," said Eddie. "We found it in the basement."

"You should have seen your face!" laughed Caroline.

"You should have seen *yours* when that man knocked at the door."

"Yeah?" said Caroline. "It takes a lot to scare *us*!"

"I'll bet you would have been scared if you'd been

with us outside your house the other night," said Wally.

"Yeah," said Jake, eager to be part of the conversation. "We were waiting for Tony to crawl back out of your basement—"

"Aha!" Beth said.

"—when the cougar came right up to us and brushed against me."

"Really?" asked Eddie.

"Wow!" cried Peter and Doug.

"We barely got Tony out in time and ran like mad," said Steve.

"Did it try to *eat* you?" asked Doug.

"I don't know what it was trying to do. Check us out, maybe," said Josh. "The sheriff says you sure don't see many around here. Dad thinks maybe someone raised it as a cub and it got loose or something, because cougars usually stay off by themselves."

Nobody spoke for a moment.

"Wouldn't it be something if we caught it?" said Steve.

"We already tried that," Jake said quickly. "We set up a trap in our backyard, with bait and everything."

"What happened?" asked Bill.

"We caught Caroline instead!" said Wally.

Everyone laughed, including Caroline.

"What were you using for a trap?" asked Steve.

"A big crate propped up on a stick," said Josh.

Steve shook his head. "You need something bigger

than that to catch a cougar! Why don't you try to trap it in our old garage?"

"Oh, sure!" said Eddie. "Dad's going to let you do that!"

"All you have to do is talk him into parking outside for a couple of nights," Steve told her.

"Yeah? And how are you going to persuade the cougar to march into your garage and wait until we call the sheriff?" asked Jake, annoyed that Steve just seemed to be taking over.

"That's the hard part," Steve admitted. "Wouldn't it be something, though, if we *did* catch it? We'd get our names in the paper and everything."

"We'd get our *picture* in the paper, along with the cougar's!" said Caroline.

"Sure," said Wally. "You could even pose with your arms around its neck, Caroline. Kiss it on the mouth if you want." Bill and Danny laughed.

But Steve looked thoughtful. "What if . . . ?" he began, and thought some more. "What if we were to leave the door of the garage open some night and put a chicken in there? And what if one of us was hiding up in the loft to pull the door shut when it happened?"

"Wait, wait, wait!" said Josh. "You're going to keep a live chicken waiting around in an open garage for—"

"A chicken from the store would probably do," said Steve.

"Even if it worked, that cougar would bound into

the garage, snatch up that chicken, and be gone before you could blink," said Beth.

"Yeah, Steve," said Jake.

"No, I've got it!" Steve said. "We buy this roasting hen, see. And then we get this really strong wire, and we fasten it tight to the chicken, so when the cougar tries to run off with it, he really has to work to get it free, and meanwhile . . ."

"Meanwhile the guy in the loft will probably have a heart attack," said Josh, and the boys laughed. All but Wally.

He could see it coming. Everyone else would set up the trap and get stuff ready, but *he'd* get stuck being the guy in the loft. It always happened that way. His brothers seemed to be able to talk him into anything, and with the Bensons on his case too, he wouldn't have a chance.

"Even if that worked, Steve, how would the guy in the loft get the door closed in time?" asked Josh.

"He'd have to do it from the window in the loft," Steve said. "I mean, the minute the cougar got inside, he'd have to be able to lean out the window and turn the latch."

"Are you nuts? That's a fifteen-foot drop," said Wally.

Tony looked over at the girls. "You haven't changed the latch on the garage door, have you?"

"No," said Beth.

The doors of the Bensons' garage were more like the doors of a barn. Above the large door was a window, in the loft. The door itself had two sections, each covering half the opening, and when they came together in the middle, a metal piece on one section fit over a latch on the other. When someone turned the latch sideways, the doors were fastened and couldn't rattle and bang in the wind.

"What a guy would need to do, see," Steve continued, "is leave just half the garage door open, and the minute the cougar got inside, he could reach down with a fishing pole, push the other half of the door shut, flip the metal piece over the latch, then knock the latch sideways using the pole."

"Yeah? *Then* what?" asked Wally.

"Then we call the sheriff and tell him you're trapped in the garage," said Tony, grinning a little.

"Dad said if any of us sneaked out again at night, he'd ground us for a week," said Wally. "Who's the lucky guy who gets to wait up in the loft for the cougar?"

"Who says it has to be a guy?" Eddie challenged him.

"Okay. It could be any one of us, except Peter or Dougie," said Tony, and he immediately turned to the two young boys. "You guys aren't to say one word to anyone about this, understand? Not a *word*!"

"We won't!" said Peter. "What do you think we are? Babies?"

There was silence for a moment. In one way, each of them wanted the job, and in another way, no one wanted it.

"I've got it!" said Jake at last. "Let's put our names in a hat, mix them up, and have somebody draw. Whoever's name is drawn is the person who will spend the night in the loft and wait for the cougar."

Beth got a piece of tablet paper and tore it into ten pieces, and all but Peter and Doug wrote their names on a piece. They folded them once and dumped them in Eddie's baseball cap. Eddie bounced the slips of paper around a little, then held the cap above Peter's head and asked him to draw one.

Peter reached up. His fingers closed around a slip of paper, and he handed it to Eddie. She unfolded it and read the name aloud: "Wally."

■ ■ ■ ■ ■ ■ ■ ■ ■ ■ ■

Twelve

■

Getting Ready

It was raining again on Thursday morning. Not a shower, not a thunderstorm. Just a steady cold rain from a steady gray sky.

"Perfect!" Eddie said to her sisters as they trooped downstairs to breakfast.

Even more perfect was that Mrs. Malloy was looking out the kitchen window saying, "Poor Mrs. Hatford! Imagine having nine boys cooped up inside your house on a day like this!"

Most of the houses in Buckman—near the college, anyway—were old and big, but they weren't big enough where it seemed to matter. A few had wraparound porches, but most had no family rooms, and rough play was not allowed in the parlors. The basement of a Victorian house was likely to be damp, with winter sleds and summer lawn furniture, rakes and shovels, and Christmas decorations all stored in its corners and along the walls. The old Benson house, where the Malloys were staying now, had a basement big enough for a Ping-Pong table but not much else.

Eddie went to the window and stood beside her mother. "Yeah, it's too bad, all right! And I invited the guys here today."

"Oh, Eddie!" said her mother. "Not with all this rain! Even if they stay in the basement, they'll be tracking mud all over the place."

"Well, it seemed the polite thing to do," Eddie answered.

"We can't very well make them stay outside," added Beth.

Mr. Malloy was checking the weather forecast in the newspaper. "Rain all week," he said. "I guess that's a chance you take over spring vacation."

Eddie gave Caroline her cue.

"I know!" Caroline said brightly. "Why couldn't we play in the garage? We could turn it into a clubhouse or something, just for the rest of the week, and all twelve of us could hang out there."

Mrs. Malloy turned from the window and looked at her husband. "You know, that's not a bad idea. I'd rather have mud out there than on my rugs."

"Okay," said Coach Malloy. "When I get home this evening, I'll park under the sycamore and they can have the run of the place."

Beth raised her eyebrows in a victory signal, and as soon as the girls concluded that Mr. Hatford had left for his job at the post office and Mrs. Hatford had gone to work at the hardware store, they phoned the boys.

Josh answered.

"We're on!" said Eddie. "Dad said we could hang out in the garage."

"Way to go!" Josh said. "We'll be over."

■

It was an hour before they got there, however. Peter and Doug looked very sleepy. Peter, in fact, was still wearing the bottom half of his pajamas, and Caroline realized that the older boys had probably forced them to get up, since they weren't supposed to be left at home alone.

But the older boys had come prepared. Jake was carrying a sleeping bag.

"Okay, guys—Peter, Doug—follow me," he said, and climbed up the ladder nailed to the inside wall of the garage. Jake disappeared through an open square in the floor above them. The old garage, like a barn, had a loft at the top, where the Bensons, and now the Malloys, stored window screens. The center of the loft was just high enough for the older boys to stand up in. Everyone followed Jake to the floor above, where he tossed the sleeping bag onto the floor, and Doug and Peter, giggling, crawled into it, more awake now than sleepy.

The others sat on the floor, listening to the rain drumming hard on the roof above.

"You know, I don't see how this is supposed to

work," said Bill. "Suppose we *do* lure the cougar into the garage. Suppose Wally *does* hear it down below. How is he supposed to crawl over to the loft window, stick the fishing pole out, push the door closed with it, flip the metal plate over the latch, and knock the latch sideways with the fishing pole—all in the *dark?*"

The boys looked at the girls, and the girls at the boys.

"He's right," said Jake finally. "It won't work. The cougar's not going to sit down and politely eat his dinner while we lock him in."

"Okay. Plan B," said Steve.

"What's plan B?" asked Eddie.

"I don't know," Steve said.

Shoulders slumped, and the loft became quiet again.

"We've got to think of something!" said Tony. "We're so close. You just *know* that cougar will be back again. If it was traipsing around when we didn't have any food out there, you know that with a fat roasting chicken, it will probably come inside long enough to grab it."

More silence. Finally Eddie said, "The only way that makes sense is for Wally to be hiding on our back porch instead of the loft. He'll have to be watching every minute, and as soon as he sees the cougar go inside, he runs over, slams the door shut, and locks it."

Wally gave a small whimper.

"Yeah, but what if Dad sees him on our porch?" said Beth.

"Listen, Wally. You'll have to hide out in the loft till we give the signal that Mom and Dad have gone upstairs," Eddie said. "We'll flick Beth's light on and off three times, and that means the coast is clear." She looked at Tony. "What time did the cougar show up the other night?"

"Between eleven and midnight."

"Then that's probably when it'll come again."

Wally looked plaintively at his brothers. "There are an awful lot of probablys in this plan. What if the cougar doesn't show up till four in the morning and I'm sound asleep? What if I'm half frozen? What if it's so dark he comes around and I don't even see him?"

"I'll sleep with Caroline tonight and leave the light on in my room," Beth said. "It shines out on the space between the house and the garage. If there's a tasty chicken inside, I don't think a little light will stop the cougar from going after it."

"Where do we get the chicken?" asked Danny.

"We'll go to the store this afternoon," Eddie told them.

■

"How much is a chicken?" Caroline asked her sisters when the boys had gone home for lunch.

"I don't know," said Beth. "A couple of dollars, maybe? How much do you have, Eddie?"

"Enough to buy a new glove before baseball tryouts, but not much more," Eddie said.

"What about you, Caroline? We already spent some money on wallpaper, remember?"

"A dollar-fifty," Caroline said.

They pooled their money and came up with three dollars and a quarter.

"How come the boys aren't forking over anything toward this chicken?" asked Caroline.

"We didn't ask them to," said Eddie. "But anyway, if we catch the cougar, it will be at *this* house, and *we'll* get our names in the paper."

"Sure: GIRLS MAULED BY COUGAR," said Caroline.

"Oh, hush," said Eddie. "Let's go to the store."

With Mrs. Malloy at the dining room table writing letters, Eddie, Beth, and Caroline put on their yellow waterproof jackets and sloshed to the store where their mother usually shopped.

"What can I get for you girls?" the butcher asked.

"How much is a chicken?" asked Eddie.

"Whole, or cut up?" said the butcher.

The girls looked at each other.

"Which do you think the cougar would prefer?" Beth whispered. "I'd think he'd like it in pieces. Easier to eat."

"But a whole chicken would seem more like nature in the raw," said Caroline.

"Whole," Eddie told the butcher.

The man named his price. "It's a nice, plump chicken," he said.

"We don't have that much," said Eddie. "How about a scrawny one?"

The butcher frowned. "I don't think your mother

would be very happy with that. I know the kind she likes."

"Well, this is sort of an unusual case. Scrawny will be fine," Eddie said.

As the girls left the store with their purchase, Beth said, "Suppose the cougar doesn't come tonight. Should we keep the chicken up in my room and try again tomorrow?"

"We'll have to," said Eddie. "We can't buy a fresh one every day. This is our only chance."

"Maybe the riper it gets, the more it will smell and attract the cougar," Beth suggested.

"And we'll have every animal in the neighborhood in our garage," said Eddie. "*That's* when the cougar will strike, I'll bet. It may not be interested in a dead chicken at all. Maybe what it really wants is live meat—a cat or dog or even a precocious nine-year-old girl. But we'll have to take that chance."

■

The boys came back later that day and they all played cards in the loft while Doug and Peter took turns tying parachutes to their G.I. Joe dolls and dropping them out the loft window.

Eddie had rigged up a light in the loft, and Mrs. Malloy let them take out a pile of old corduroy cushions to sit on, so the loft had become a more inviting place.

As a surprise, Mrs. Hatford ordered some Kentucky Fried Chicken to be delivered to them in the garage, and the twelve had a boisterous picnic, trading pieces of chicken for extra biscuits, or bartering for an extra can of pop.

"Boys," Coach Malloy called out, around seven. "The Hatfords want you home now, so pack it up."

Up in the loft, Eddie crawled around gathering up all the leftover chicken bones and put them in a sack for the garbage. One by one the Malloys and Hatfords and Bensons climbed down the ladder into the garage below.

"You'd better come on home, Wally, and sneak back later," said Josh. "If Mom sees you around for a while, she probably won't discover you're missing later."

"Yeah," said Jake. "If Josh or I were gone, she'd know right away we were up to something. And if Peter wasn't there, she'd notice. But if Bill and Danny are in your room and your bed has a couple pillows in it, she won't think to ask. When you're the middle child, you can get away with murder."

The boys went off down the hill toward the swinging bridge, and the girls went back inside.

"I've got that roasting chicken in my closet," said Beth. "When do we put it in the garage?"

"Not until Wally gets back, that's for sure," said Eddie.

■

Around ten o'clock, just after her father had locked up for the night, Caroline saw the beam of a flashlight bobbing about in the loft and knew that Wally had come back and was waiting for their signal.

"Good grief," said Eddie. "If Mom or Dad look out and see that light, they're going to go out there and send Wally home. Caroline, go tell him to turn off the flashlight, will you?"

"What about the chicken?" Caroline asked.

"It's under the sink now. As soon as the folks go upstairs, I'll sneak out and wire it to a pole at the back of the garage," Eddie said.

Caroline heard her parents' footsteps going upstairs. She took her jacket off a peg by the back door, silently pulled the door open, and stepped out into the cold night air. The light from Beth's window made a large square of yellow light in the space between house and garage. It wasn't so cold out; Wally shouldn't complain about having to do guard duty on the back porch. If *her* name had been picked out of the hat, she would have done it without any grumbling at all.

She had just started down the porch steps when something caught her eye. She stopped, one foot in the air, motionless, staring hard through the darkness just to the left of the garage. And then she saw what it was and her heart almost stopped: the cougar.

The animal came stealthily out from the evergreens, sniffed at the air, and looked about, its tail twitching. Then, hugging the side of the garage, staying in the shadows, it moved silently to the open door and stopped again, eyes and ears alert. And suddenly it darted inside.

The KFC! That must be what the big cat was after,

Caroline thought wildly, thinking of the chicken bones in the sack at the back of the garage.

She didn't even stop to think. Noiselessly she leaped off the steps, her heart pounding in her ears, rushed to the garage, flung the door closed, and latched it.

Thirteen

■

In the Loft

Wally followed his brothers into the house. It was probably true what Jake had said, that his mom wouldn't miss Wally at all. She'd miss Peter, being the youngest, and Jake and Josh, being the oldest, and twins at that, but Wally usually got lost in the shuffle. He imagined that if he never came home at all, she might look at Dad someday and say, "Didn't we used to have a son in fourth grade? I wonder whatever happened to him?" and Dad would say, "His name was Wally, wasn't it? Or was it Winston, or Warren?"

"I've run the bathwater, Peter," Mrs. Hatford called. "Do you and Doug want to take a bath together? The rest of you boys can bathe tonight, or you can shower in the morning, if you'd rather."

"We'll shower in the morning," said Jake.

Wally went up to his room with Bill and Danny, but Jake and Steve came crowding in after them.

"You have to go talk to her, Wally. *Say* something so she'll remember you were here," Jake insisted.

With a sigh, Wally went back downstairs. Mother was busy making a grocery list in the kitchen.

"I've never seen food disappear so fast in all my life," she said to no one in particular. "You'd think we were feeding a pride of hungry lions."

Trying not to think of lions, Wally cleared his throat.

"What is it?" his mother asked, scarcely looking up. She was checking how much bread was left in the bread drawer.

"I think maybe we need more blankets in my room," Wally said, not knowing what else to say.

"Well, you know where they are. Help yourself," his mother replied. And then, "If they're all taken, Wally, get the afghan off the couch. Come to think of it, we've used every pillow in the house too."

"Well, good night," Wally said. "I guess I'll go to bed."

"Bread . . . eggs . . . orange juice . . . What?" Mrs. Hatford asked distractedly.

"Good night," Wally repeated.

"Oh. Good night. Don't forget to open your window," his mother said. She was a firm believer in fresh air, especially when nine boys with smelly sneakers were all residing under her roof.

Wally went slowly back upstairs.

"Okay," Josh whispered, pulling him into the twins' bedroom, where the other boys were waiting, all but Peter and Doug. "You'd better take Dad's old parka with you, just in case you get cold. Flashlight . . . whistle . . ."

"Whistle? What's that for?" asked Wally.

"I don't know . . . just in case," Josh said. Wally felt sick to his stomach, but with everyone watching, he dared not show it.

"Maybe one of us better go with him," said Josh.

"No!" said Wally. "I can do this myself."

He was ready at last, with flashlight, whistle, popcorn, water bottle, and two PayDay candy bars.

"If you trap him, come back *immediately* and tell us!" Steve insisted as Danny and Bill studied Wally admiringly. "We want to be there when the photographers show up."

"Just throw sticks at our window or something, and we'll come right down," said Josh.

They hustled Wally over to the window and helped him climb onto the branch of the tree. Wally felt like a fireman in protective gear sliding down a pole in the firehouse. Except that there was no truck to ride at the bottom. No buddies to go with him. He was wearing so many clothes to keep warm that even if the cougar did show up, Wally could hardly run with the two pairs of pants he had on, the three shirts, the heavy socks.

The clouds were streaking across the sky, blown by the March wind, and once in a while the moon shone through.

Wally crossed the bridge, his hiking boots making dull thuds on the boards, and a phrase kept ringing in his head: *We who are about to die salute you.* He wondered where that came from. Then he remembered: It was what Roman gladiators were supposed to have said to the emperor before they fought in the Colosseum. Or right before they faced the lions, he wasn't sure which.

Every snap of a twig, every swish of a branch overhead, sounded like a cougar to him, a sound a cougar might make if it were stalking him. He had no business in the world being out here at night alone, he knew. But how could he back out in front of the Bensons?

As he started up the hill toward the garage, he thought for a minute that he felt the breath of a cougar on his neck. He wheeled about, gasping, slapping at the air, only to discover that a piece of the lining of his dad's wool hunting cap was dangling down his neck.

The light from Beth's window illuminated the ground beyond the house, and he knew he was supposed to wait until the light went on and off three times before he left the loft and hunkered down on their back porch. One of the two garage doors had been propped open with a brick so that it wouldn't bang in the breeze. Mr. Malloy's car was parked outside under the sycamore.

Wally could still smell the KFC as he entered, and he wished he had a piece of it now. He thought for a minute of rummaging about in the sack there on the floor to see if he could salvage something, but decided against it. Laboriously he climbed the rungs to the loft and lowered himself in his bulky clothes onto one of the cushions. Lying on his back, he turned on the flashlight and directed the beam at the low ceiling. He made larger and larger circles, then reversed directions, and spiraling downward, made the circles smaller and smaller.

When he tired of that, he turned off the flashlight and rolled over on his stomach, watching the window of the Malloys' house. It seemed weird that only a year ago he had been hanging out with the Bensons up here, and now the Bensons were over in his house, in his room, and a bunch of girls were in the Bensons' bedrooms. And here he was at ten o'clock at night, waiting for a cougar to show up on Island Avenue. Was he nuts or was he nuts?

He thought again about school. The week was almost over and he hadn't come up with one idea of what he could try that he'd never done before. Well, at least now he was doing something that was half crazy. Even if the cougar didn't show, he was probably the only boy in his class who had spent spring vacation waiting for it. But how could he write about that?

One by one, the other lights began to go off in the house, until only the light from Beth's window remained. Wally expected one of the girls to come out soon with the chicken, but when minutes passed and no one came, he turned on the flashlight again and began making zigzag lines along the wall.

He thought he heard a noise and paused. Was it a huff? A puff? A grunt? A growl?

He turned off the flashlight again and looked out the window. Caroline was standing perfectly still on the back steps, one hand on the railing, one foot in midair. She looked like a statue in a park, the way horses were often sculpted with one raised hoof.

Hey, Caroline, what are you? A horse? Wally wanted to call out, but of course he didn't.

Suddenly, below him, he heard the sound of a paper sack rustling, and just as suddenly, Caroline came rushing down the steps and over to the garage.

Wally heard the bang of the garage door, and the click of the metal latch.

He stopped breathing, because the next thing he heard was a huffing sound from below—a soft, almost inaudible pacing, and every so often a *whump,* as though someone, or something, was throwing its body against the door of the garage, as though someone, or something, was trying to get out.

And then Wally knew: he was trapped in the garage with the cougar.

He started to yell out the window to Caroline, but his voice stuck in his throat. Was he *crazy?* Did he want the cougar to know he was up here?

Wally's heart pounded so violently, he thought it would beat right through his chest. As long as he was quiet, he told himself, as long as he hardly even breathed, the big cat would let him be. Maybe. And then his heart almost stopped a second time: *cat*. A cougar was a lion, a cat. And cats could climb.

The chicken hadn't even been put out yet! The cougar must have smelled the leftover KFC. It would be angry that there was nothing much left to eat. Angry that it had been trapped. And if there was no whole chicken to eat . . . maybe a boy would do.

It didn't have to see Wally, didn't have to hear him. All it had to do was get a whiff of Wally Hatford and it would be climbing those rungs to the loft in an instant.

Wally's mouth was open in terror. This was not what he wanted to do for Miss Applebaum. This is not the way he wanted to die! He had always thought death might come by avalanche on a mountain climbing trek, or in a fighter plane downed in battle or that he'd be a sailor sunk at sea. He'd thought he'd be given a hero's funeral, with drums and bagpipes and long rows of mourners following his casket.

He did not want to be found torn limb from limb in the loft of an old garage, with all his fingers and toes nibbled off. He did not want his parents saying, "Didn't we have a boy who looked something like that—before the cougar ate his chin?"

Caroline had to know he was up here! Wally stared desperately out the window, but all he could see was the back door of the house after Caroline had run inside and closed it. Was she going to wait till morning to tell anybody?

Whump, went the sound from below.

Huff, huff, huff.

Whump . . . whump . . . whump.

Wally closed his eyes. *We who are about to die salute you.*

■ ■ ■ ■ ■ ■ ■ ■ ■ ■ ■ ■ ■

Fourteen

■

911

Caroline banged the door shut behind her, her heart exploding in her chest, her eyes huge. Should she get Eddie? Tell her father? Call 911? *What?*

She didn't do any of those. She screamed. She just opened her mouth and let loose with the most piercing, ear-splitting scream she could manage. Then she took a deep breath and waited.

She didn't have to wait long. There was a two- or three-second pause, and then the house was filled with the sound of running feet.

"Caroline?" came her father's voice from upstairs. "Where are you? What's happened?"

In panic, Caroline screamed again.

"Caroline!" cried her mother.

"Hey, Caroline, what's the matter?" yelled Eddie, and then they were all flocking into the kitchen.

"The cougar!" Caroline gasped. "It's in the garage."

"What?" cried Coach Malloy.

"Where's Wally?" asked Beth.

"He's in the garage too," said Caroline.

"What?" yelled their father. He ran to the back door and peered out the window. The garage door was closed. The night was still. He turned around and stared at Caroline. "How do you know?"

"I saw it go in, and shut the door behind it, and *Wally's* in there! Up in the loft!"

Coach Malloy grabbed his jacket, and then Eddie's baseball bat lying next to the door. "Jean, call 911," he instructed, and opened the back door.

"Wally?" he yelled. "Wally?"

No answer.

Coach Malloy whirled around and faced Caroline again. "What is he doing in the garage at this time of night?"

"W-waiting for the cougar," explained Eddie excitedly. "We were trying to catch it, and we did!"

"Girls!" cried their mother, but then she was speaking into the phone. "Yes. Six-eleven Island Avenue. We have a boy trapped in a garage with a cougar. . . . Yes, a *cougar*! Oh, please hurry!" She hung up.

"Wally?" Mr. Malloy yelled again, standing in the clearing between the house and the garage.

And then a face appeared at the loft's open window.

"Wally!" everyone cried at once.

Whump came from inside the garage, as the cougar threw its weight against the door. *Whump!*

"D-Dad!" cried Beth. "What if it gets out?"

"What if it gets me?" croaked Wally in a stage whisper. "Can you get me down?"

"Don't jump!" Mr. Malloy warned. "It's too far. Eddie, get the tall stepladder."

"It's in the garage," said Eddie.

"The *folding* ladder?"

She nodded.

There was the distant sound of a siren.

"The police are on the way," Mrs. Malloy said.

"Can cougars climb ladders?" Wally asked plaintively. "Because if they can, it's going to come up here."

"Do you have anything you could put over the opening to the loft, Wally?" Mr. Malloy said.

"I already put a window screen over the hole, but it doesn't fit," Wally said, and leaned even farther out the window.

"Don't jump!" Coach Malloy called again. "Here they are now!"

A patrol car, lights flashing, came speeding across the road bridge at the end of Island Avenue, followed by a fire truck and the rescue vehicle. As they rolled into the driveway, lights came on in neighboring houses.

Two policemen got out and came over.

"You sure you've got the cougar in there?" one asked.

"I'm not sure of anything, but my daughter says we do. And there's a kid up there who needs to come down," Coach Malloy said, pointing toward Wally, who was now sitting on the window ledge, one leg dangling over the side.

Whump, thump, came from inside the garage, followed by loud huffing.

"Pleeeease?" came Wally's plaintive cry.

"Get that kid down," the policeman said to the firemen. They removed a ladder from their truck and braced it against the side of the garage. Another car pulled up and Tom Hatford got out.

"Hey, Tom, you the sheriff's deputy tonight?" one of the policemen called.

"Yeah, I'm on duty," Mr. Hatford said. "What have we got here? What's this about a cougar?"

"Girl says she's got a cougar trapped in the garage, and there's a boy in there with him. We're getting him out right now," the second officer said.

Mr. Hatford looked over to where the firemen were putting up the ladder. His mouth dropped. "Wally?" he said.

"Dad?" said Wally.

Mr. Hatford ran over to the barn and stood staring up at his son.

"Hold on there, now," said the fireman who was climbing the ladder. "You're one brave kid, and you're doing just fine."

When he reached the top, he guided Wally's foot off the sill and onto the second rung. Then the fireman backed down, with Wally in front of him.

Tom Hatford walked over to George Malloy. "If I live to be a hundred, I will never understand our kids," he said.

"We won't even *live* to be a hundred, Tom, with *them* around! I lost a year of my life tonight just *thinking* about Wally in there with that animal," said Coach Malloy. "'Trying to catch a cougar,'" they said. But both men gave Wally a hug when he reached the ground.

Whump! Whump! The sounds from inside the garage were getting louder, and everyone could hear the cougar's breathing.

"Anybody got a tranquilizer gun?" one of the policemen asked. He looked over at the men from the rescue squad.

"'Fraid not," one of them said.

A gaggle of boys appeared, running up the hill from the river. Jake and Josh and Danny and Bill, Steve and Tony and Doug—and Peter, still wearing his bunny slippers. Mrs. Hatford, with an overcoat thrown on top of her nightgown, was not far behind. They got there just in time to see Wally descend the ladder.

"Wow! What happened?" asked Steve.

"We got the cougar!" yelled Caroline. "I locked him in the garage." And then she lost control. "Oh, it was so awful! He almost had me by the throat, but—"

"Caroline! Can it!" warned Eddie.

The policeman spoke into his radio, asking the dispatcher to send the animal control truck with a tranquilizer gun. Then a car pulled up with a photographer and a reporter from the newspaper, and they came right over to where Wally and Caroline were standing.

"Who actually captured the cougar?" the reporter asked as the photographer adjusted his camera.

"We all did," said Eddie. "We all planned it, even though Caroline was the one who locked the garage door. So we all get the credit."

"Who's *we*?" the reporter asked, and everyone took turns telling the story.

The photographer arranged the twelve kids in two rows outside the door of the garage and took a picture, then another and another, and asked the Hatfords and Malloys for permission to print them.

"I guess I can speak for the Bensons, since we've got their boys for the night," Mrs. Hatford told them.

Whump! Thump!

The photographer suddenly backed away and stared at the closed doors of the garage.

The animal control truck pulled up.

"Okay, now, I want everybody up on the porch," said one of the men from the truck after talking with the officer. "I'm going to go up the ladder into the loft and see if I can fire a tranquilizer dart from up there. I need you officers to cover for me in case, when we open the door later, the cat's not down."

Up went the man with the tranquilizer gun, and for some time nothing happened.

"Can't get him in my sights," he called out to a fireman who stood on the ladder outside the loft window. "Keeps pacing. He's nervous, all right."

Finally there was a pop as the gun went off.

"Got his thigh," the man called. And then, a few minutes later, "Okay. He's down. You can open the door."

Caroline and her sisters stood behind the railing of the small back porch with the nine boys from across the river. When the garage doors were opened at last, out came the cougar, carried in a sling by four sturdy men, who placed it in the back of the panel truck.

Everyone streamed off the porch to see the cougar, and the Hatford and Benson boys went down the line giving high fives to all the Malloy girls. The Malloy girls went down the line giving high fives to all the guys.

"Do you think we know even one tenth of what these kids are up to half the time?" Mrs. Hatford asked Mrs. Malloy.

"I doubt it, and I don't think I want to know," Caroline's mother replied. "How do they *think* of these things? How can they possibly get into so much trouble without our knowing?"

"That wasn't trouble at all!" Caroline crowed. "We caught the cougar and saved Buckman!" She dramatically raised her arms to the sky.

"And next thing we know, you'll say you saved Western civilization," said her mother. "Come down from whatever planet you're on, Caroline Lenore, and go to bed. It's been quite a day."

Fifteen

■

The Great Hullabaloo

COUGAR CAPTURED BY KIDS, ran the banner headline in the newspaper the next morning. The boys had the pages spread out across the breakfast table.

Oh, how Wally wished they were in school right now so that he could tell all about it! There under the headline was a photo of twelve kids, including Peter in his bunny slippers. The Benson boys were back, and together (well, the girls did help a little) they had captured the beast that had stalked Buckman since last November.

He imagined standing up before Miss Applebaum and the whole class and recounting the terrifying ordeal in the garage. He had done something he had never done before—something no one else would ever do again, probably. Then he thought of Caroline, who would stand up next and tell how she—Caroline

117

Lenore Malloy—had captured the beast single-handedly, and his own part didn't seem quite so wonderful.

"Man oh man oh man!" said Steve. "I wish this story would make the paper down in Georgia! Wouldn't we be something then!"

"Hey, look at the grin on your face!" Danny said, ribbing Bill as they studied the photo. "And you weren't even there when the cougar was caught."

"Well, neither were you!" Bill shot back.

"But we were all in on the planning, so we all get the credit," said Tony.

"It was my idea in the first place," said Steve.

They had all read the story, but Mr. Hatford read it again, this time aloud:

"Police, firemen, rescue squad, and animal control officials were called to the residence of George Malloy, 611 Island Avenue, last night when one of his daughters trapped a cougar in their garage.

"A fourth grader, Caroline Malloy, 9, witnessed the cougar entering the open door of the garage on the property they rent from the Bensons and locked the animal inside. Wally Hatford, also in fourth grade, was in the loft of the garage at the time and had to be rescued by firemen. Jack Werner, of Animal Control, then entered the loft through the window and tranquilized the agitated animal.

"The cougar is believed to be the same elusive creature, dubbed the 'abaguchie,' which has stalked residents of Buckman for the past several months. It is thought to be responsible for the deaths of several area pets.

"The Malloy girls, in conjunction with the Hatford boys and the visiting Benson brothers, presently of Georgia, had hatched a scheme for capturing the cougar. Authorities believe the animal was drawn to the garage by the smell of a fried chicken dinner the children had consumed several hours earlier in the garage.

" 'We don't condone any private citizen taking it upon himself to capture a wild animal,' Officer Lou Hanson said. 'Cougars are dangerous, and although they usually live solitary lives and keep their distance from humans, more and more wild animals are roaming closer to towns as man encroaches on their natural habitat. Cougars, of course, are rare in West Virginia, and it's possible that this one was owned by someone who had no license to harbor a wild animal and who did not want to notify authorities when the cougar escaped. We're just grateful that the ordeal is over and no one was hurt, but we've got to give the kids credit for quick thinking.' "

Mr. Hatford, however, wasn't about to credit anybody. Now that his son was safely home again, he thought of all that *might* have happened.

"Wally, what were you *thinking*?" he demanded.

"That I was about to die," Wally answered simply.

"The cougar could have *killed* you! Maimed you forever!" Mr. Hatford looked around the table at his three oldest sons. "I don't know whether to ground you for a month or send the whole lot of you to Siberia!"

It was Jake who showed quick thinking now. "How about if we put in ten hours at the police station, mopping floors or washing windows or whatever they need us to do?" he suggested. *Any*thing was better than being grounded.

"Sold!" said his father. "I'll tell them you're coming. But what I don't understand is if you boys were going to try a cockeyed stunt like that, why Wally? Why not one of you older boys?"

"We drew names," said Jake, "and Wally got picked."

Mrs. Hatford suddenly swooped down and put her arms around Wally as he took another bite of Cocoa Puffs. "Oh, Wally, if anything had happened to you, I don't know what I would have done," she murmured. "I'd miss you so much!"

Wally stared straight ahead as she planted a kiss on his cheek and his brothers giggled. She'd miss him? She would actually *miss* him? She *almost* sounded as though she'd miss him more than anyone else in the family.

Mr. and Mrs. Benson arrived shortly after that, having heard the early-morning news. Mrs. Benson was still in her slippers.

"My gracious, is everyone all right?" she cried.

"We put them together for five days, Tom, and look what happens!" said Mr. Benson, giving each of his sons a grateful hug. "They're in the newspaper. On the radio! TV! The works!"

"TV?" yelped Danny delightedly.

"It was on the early news, and they'll repeat it again at eight-thirty," said his mother.

"Well, I'm staying home from work today, so I'll see it too!" Mrs. Hatford turned on the TV and they watched six commercials before the local news was repeated.

"The cougar captured yesterday in the garage at six-eleven Island Avenue has been checked over by wildlife experts and is on its way to a remote area of the Smoky Mountains, where it will be set free," the commentator said. "Its capture was part of a scheme by twelve local children to trap the animal, and though things didn't go quite according to plan, the cougar was locked in the garage long enough for animal control officials to tranquilize it and remove it from the premises. Buckman salutes the twelve plucky kids who hatched the scheme, but the final word from the mayor is, 'It's okay this time, but don't let it happen again.' "

"Can we go to the Malloys' now?" Steve asked. "We want to show them the newspaper."

"The Malloys read newspapers too, you know," Mr. Benson said. "Why don't we take all you kids to the movies?"

"We'd really rather see the Malloys," said Tony.

"Then yes, by all means, *go!*" Mrs. Hatford said, glancing at the continuing rain outside the window. And then, to Mr. and Mrs. Benson, she added, "They are so wired this morning, I won't be able to keep them in the house. Please stay and visit—we can have the kitchen all to ourselves."

Grabbing their jackets, the boys ran outside into the misty rain and headed for the footbridge. The water had been rising in the Buckman River and was only six feet below the bridge.

"If it keeps on raining like this, the river will flood," said Danny. "Remember that time it got up almost as high as the footbridge?"

"Come on!" Steve said. "I see the girls outside."

Indeed, the Malloys were waiting for them, standing out in the yard in their yellow slickers. They looked like crossing guards, Wally thought. He had only come over here because the other guys wanted to come, but he knew that Caroline would be unbearable.

She was.

"Did you see? Did you see?" she called excitedly, running forward to meet them. "My picture's right there on the front page, and—"

"We're *all* on the front page, Caroline," said Eddie. "Pipe down, will you?"

"So, what do you think? Was it a good idea or was it a good *idea*!" Steve bragged.

"Okay, so it was a good idea!" said Jake irritably. Now *Steve* was getting unbearable.

"I didn't even get a chance to put the chicken out," said Eddie. "The cougar must have been really hungry to go for those leftover food scraps and bones." The twelve of them moved inside the garage to keep dry.

"Wally, weren't you *scared* up there in the loft?" Beth asked him. "I'd have been terrified."

"Oh, I don't know," said Wally. "I figured I'd get down sooner or later."

"Weren't *you* scared, Caroline, when you shut the door?" asked Bill.

Caroline dramatically placed her hand over her heart. "Absolutely, positively terrified!" she answered. "My entire life flashed before my eyes. All the roles on Broadway I would never play. 'Do it for the good of Buckman,' I told myself, even though I might be clawed to death."

"Oh, brother!" murmured Tony.

∎

All day, neighborhood kids came by the garage to see where the cougar had been trapped. They wanted to climb up into the loft to see where Wally had been hiding, to see the window where the animal control man had climbed inside. Caroline sat at the back of the garage holding court like a queen, and all she would say when friends asked if she had been scared was, "Absolutely, positively terrified."

"She's sickening," said Beth. "*Do* something, Eddie!"

"Hey, Caroline," Eddie called. "You know what we just found out? You may have RM disease. Anyone who is anywhere near a wild animal, like a cougar, is susceptible to an airborne virus that's sometimes fatal. You were probably closer than anyone."

Caroline stopped bragging and stared at her sisters. "I wasn't as close as the animal control people."

"They've all been vaccinated against it," Eddie said. "You weren't."

Caroline's face paled. "What are the symptoms?"

"Rapid heartbeat, excitability, flushed face, sweating hands, delusions of grandeur . . ."

"Oh, my gosh, Eddie, what will I do? How will I know if I've got it?" Caroline cried in alarm.

"You'll have to go to the hospital and get a bunch of tests. They stick a tube down your throat and take about twenty blood samples, and put wires in your ears and everything."

"What *is* RM disease?" Caroline asked, quickly getting to her feet and ready to run inside the house.

"Running-mouth disease," said Eddie, and everyone laughed. Caroline glowered at her sister and sat back down, arms folded across her chest.

Wally laughed too, and looked around at the guys, glad it was all over and they could enjoy the rest of spring vacation. The boys were sitting on one side of the garage, the girls on the other. All except Steve and Eddie. They were sitting together, side by side, and they were practically *touching*, Wally noticed. After all this, one of the Bensons had fallen for Eddie Malloy! He couldn't believe it!

Sixteen

■

Goodbye

"This was the most exciting spring vacation we ever had," Beth declared on Saturday as the girls woke to still more rain on the roof. "Even though I feel like I'm turning into a mushroom. Will this rain never stop?"

"I'm going to miss Steve, I think, when the Bensons go back to Georgia," said Eddie.

"What?" cried Caroline.

"I will. He's the nicest Benson of all."

"Well, *I'm* going to miss all the excitement," said Caroline, "but at least I finished my school assignment, and the newspaper story makes a new page for my résumé when I become an actress. Then they'll *see* that I can play incredibly brave roles onstage. I'll bet I'm the only girl in the whole United States who ever locked a cougar in a garage."

"I don't know about that, but I'll bet you're the only girl in the whole United States who goes around bragging so much about it," Beth told her.

"You don't understand, Beth! Actresses need all the attention they can get to stay in the public eye. It's not wrong to go around tooting my own horn."

"No, but you don't have to *lean* on it!" said Eddie dryly.

The girls had scarcely brushed their teeth when there was a knock on the back door. Eddie opened it.

"Steve!" she said.

He smiled a little shyly. "Just came over to say goodbye. We'll be leaving in a little while."

"Goodbye?" said Eddie. "Why, you just got here, practically." She saw the other boys coming across the yard behind him.

"I know. But Mom wants a day to get the laundry done and everything before we start back to school," Steve said. "So we're going home this morning."

Eddie and her sisters stepped out on the back porch.

"We didn't get to do half the stuff we really wanted," Caroline complained.

"We didn't either," Doug piped up. "We were going to wave sheets in front of your window and make you think it was ghosts."

"Shut up, Dougie," Bill told him.

"And Steve was going to slip a note under your door," said Peter.

"Shut *up*!" said Steve. His face turned pink.

Eddie's did as well.

"Have you decided whether or not to move back to Buckman?" Beth asked Tony.

"I don't know. Dad hasn't said. What about you?"

"We don't know either. Maybe it depends on what *your* dad does," said Beth.

"I guess there's not room for two football coaches at the college," said Eddie. "What they should do is start a baseball team or something."

"Yeah," said Steve. "That would be neat."

There was a blast from a horn across the river.

"We've got to go," Tony said. He looked at Jake. "You guys better write to us, okay?"

"Yeah, now that we've met the Whomper, the Weirdo, and the Crazie, you have to keep us posted on what they do," said Danny, and he and Bill grinned.

"That's *us,* I suppose? Ha, ha, ha!" said Eddie.

"Hope you make the team, Eddie," said Steve, smiling at her.

"I'll write you if I do," she said.

"Hope you don't hear any more ghosts, Beth," said Tony.

"Hope you get laryngitis, Caroline, and can't talk for a month!" said Bill. The boys laughed, and so did Caroline.

The horn sounded again, and the Benson boys set off down the hill beside the Hatfords.

"I never thought I'd miss those guys, but I will," said Beth.

"I never thought I'd miss boys at all, but I do," said Eddie.

"But isn't it nice just to be sisters again and not have *them* coming over every day, climbing all over the loft and tracking mud up on the porch with their stinky shoes?" said Caroline.

"No," answered Beth and Eddie together.

■

That night, Caroline lay in bed thinking about school, and about how she might be asked to describe for the class how she had caught the cougar. *I know!* she thought. *Wally and I can do it together! He can stand up on Miss Applebaum's desk and pretend it's the loft, and I'll be down below* . . . She felt herself drifting off into a dream about cougars and firemen and Wally Hatford when she suddenly heard a *tap . . . tappity-tap . . . tap . . . tap . . . tap . . . tap.*

She opened her eyes.

Tap . . . tap . . . tap, it came again.

Caroline turned and looked at the clock. Almost midnight.

Tap . . . tap . . . tap. The noise was coming from the wall behind her bed.

Caroline got up and put her mouth to the floor register. "Okay, you guys, I know you're down there," she called softly.

Tap . . . tappity-tap. The noise continued.

Bolder now because of her encounter with the cougar, Caroline decided not to tell her sisters but to investigate on her own. Undoubtedly, one of the Hatford boys had crawled back through the basement window, as Tony had done before, and was tapping on the water pipes to make her think the house was haunted for sure.

She slipped into the hall and down the stairs and got a flashlight from the kitchen. Then, without turning on any lights, she opened the basement door and stealthily started down the stairs. One step . . . two steps . . . three steps . . . four . . .

She waited until she got to the bottom before she snapped on the flashlight. The furnace pipes made grotesque shadows on the wall, like long fingers against the cinder block.

"I know you're down here," Caroline repeated, a little less boldly than before. Holding the flashlight out in front of her, she began moving around the corner of the basement toward the Ping-Pong table.

Step by step, closer and closer. When she got right over to the table, she directed the beam of the flashlight toward the basement window. Closed. Locked, in fact. She turned slowly and pointed the light in all directions, but she saw no one. No one at all.

Tap . . . tap . . . tap. She could still hear the ghostly tapping from somewhere. Then she heard another sound. Footsteps. The creak of the floor above.

Step by step, step by step . . . closer and closer. Now the footsteps were crossing the kitchen floor. Now they were at the door of the basement. Now they were coming down the basement steps. . . .

"Helllp!" screeched Caroline.

"Good grief!" called her father. "Caroline Lenore, what in the world are you up to?"

"Oh, Dad! I heard a noise. . . . A ghostly tapping . . . And I thought the house was haunted, or the boys were back, or—"

"We've got a leak in the roof from all the rain. Water's running down inside the wall and hitting a heat duct, that's all," her father said.

Beth and Eddie appeared behind him in their pajamas and bare feet.

"What is it? What's the matter?" they asked.

"Your sister's imagination is on the loose, that's what," said Coach Malloy. "Caroline, could you possibly make the effort to forget about ghosts for one night?"

"It won't be easy," said Caroline.

"Do you think it's too much to ask that you stay in your bed until morning?"

"I suppose not," said Caroline.

"Do you think your father could have one night of peace and quiet before spring vacation ends?" he asked.

"I'll try," said Caroline.

"Then get the heck to bed," said her father, and she did.

■

On Monday morning, Wally came out of the house with his brothers and found the Malloy girls waiting for them at the end of the bridge. They were used to walking to school together now, and Jake and Josh fell in beside Beth and Eddie, while Peter skipped happily on ahead. That left Wally, of course, to walk with

Caroline, who had a sickening smile on her face. A scary smile. A sickening, scary smile that could mean only one thing: trouble.

"Good *morning*, Wally!" she said, moving up beside him.

"No," said Wally. "Whatever it is, no!"

"I have an idea for our spring assignment, and I'll bet you can guess what it is."

"The answer is no," said Wally.

"Everyone is going to ask you about it anyway, so you might as well get up and tell the class."

"No," said Wally, but even then he knew he was doomed.

"We'll not just *tell* about capturing the cougar, Wally, we'll *show* it. We can use Miss Applebaum's desk for the loft, and I'll be down below, and maybe we could get Peter to be the cougar, and—"

We who are about to die salute you, Wally said to himself, smiling a little, but he kept his eyes on the road ahead.

■ ■ ■ ■ ■ ■ ■ ■ ■ ■ ■ ■

About the Author

Phyllis Reynolds Naylor enjoys writing about the Hatford boys and the Malloy girls because the books take place in her husband's home state, West Virginia. The town of Buckman in the stories is really Buckhannon, where her husband spent most of his growing-up years. There are now seven books in the series — *The Boys Start the War, The Girls Get Even, Boys Against Girls, The Girls' Revenge, A Traitor Among the Boys, A Spy Among the Girls,* and *The Boys Return*—and Mrs. Naylor plans to write five more, one for each month that the girls are in Buckman, though who knows whether or not they will move back to Ohio at the end?

Phyllis Reynolds Naylor is the author of more than a hundred books, a number of which are set in West Virginia, including the Newbery Award–winning *Shiloh* and the other two books in the Shiloh trilogy, *Shiloh Season* and *Saving Shiloh.* She and her husband live in Bethesda, Maryland.